GHOSTS
IN OUR
BACKYARD

GHOSTS
IN OUR
BACKYARD

THE RAMSAYS'
REAL-LIFE ENCOUNTERS
WITH THE SUPERNATURAL

ALISHA 'PRITI' KIRPALANI

HarperCollins *Publishers* India

First published in India by
HarperCollins *Publishers* in 2021
A-75, Sector 57, Noida, Uttar Pradesh 201301, India
www.harpercollins.co.in

2 4 6 8 10 9 7 5 3 1

P-ISBN: 978-93-9032-760-7
E-ISBN: 978-93-9032-761-4

Typeset in 11.5/15.5 Adobe Garamond at
Manipal Digital Systems, Manipal

Printed and bound in India by
Manipal Technologies Limited, Manipal

This book is dedicated, first and foremost, to my mother, Asha. This one's for you, Maa.

For staying up with me through every exam.
For the horror movies we binge-watched together.
For the comforting chats deep into the night.
For being my light in the darkness.
For teaching me about duty, charity and honesty.
For your eternal patience, positivity and resilience.
For being my first sanctuary.
For that tenderness in your hug
that always feels like home.
Thank you, Maa, till my dying breath.
And beyond.

To my father, Deva, who does everything he possibly can to see me happy. Thank you, Daddy, for all your support and sacrifice, while trying so hard to do your best for me.

To my grandparents, Naana and Naani, my maternal uncles, The Ramsay Brothers, my maternal aunt, Kamla Maasi, and their families for all the unforgettable childhood memories of love and pampering.

To my paternal grandparents, Dada and Bhabi, for providing us with everything and working so hard so we had it easy.

To the two parts of my soul, my most perfect creations, my girls, Sascha and Tiana, who I hope to make proud just as I am of them.

Last but never the least, to my soulmate, Johnny, the man behind the woman I am today. Thank you from my heart for coming into my life and giving birth to a better, happier me. Without you, there would be neither us nor me.

Contents

Who Am I?

I believe in the spirit world.
I have a trident on my palm.
I was born in a car outside a crematorium.
I am a daughter of the Ramsays, the first family of Bollywood
horror films.
I believe in ghosts because I have seen them.
So has my mother.
So has my daughter.
Who am I?
I am the one who will give voice to the whispers of the world
beyond ours.
That world where our loved ones who have passed away
watch over us,
as the unloved others watch us.
Sometimes the dead reach out, crossing over the impossible.
Their souls wander endlessly, some tormented with suffering,
some tender with yearning.
Their stories must be told.
They must be heard.
I am their storyteller.

Growing Up Among
the Ramsays

In *Housefull 4*, actor Nawazuddin Siddiqui plays an exorcist called Ramsay Baba. I watched the Akshay Kumar-starrer and realized just how much my maternal family – the Ramsays – has contributed to Bollywood.

The Ramsay name is synonymous with horror and the paranormal, and has frequently been mentioned across films. To be remembered over decades as the pioneers of horror in Bollywood is a testimony to the Ramsay achievements. The Ramsays have often been tagged as 'B-grade' filmmakers, but theirs was a purposeful endeavour to make films for the masses and on a limited budget; they never claimed to be making classics. They wanted people to experience fear through their films, and they wanted to make money while doing this. When they started, they could not have imagined that their films would eventually gain such a cult following.

Unfortunately, most of the brothers and their father passed away before they could see the renewed interest in their trademark genre – horror. The surviving ones have the same question on their lips, 'Why the interest in us now, after all these years?'

The answer to that question is fairly simple. As my mother proudly used to say, 'In Hollywood, horror was Hitchcock and in India, horror was the Ramsays.'

That statement holds true even today.

The Ramsays were unique in their approach and vision of films. In their early years of film-making, the whole family went on a holiday to Kashmir and lived on a houseboat for over three months. Under the strict supervision of F.U. Ramsay (hereafter, F.U.), the sons got a crash course in various aspects of filmmaking, a skill they taught themselves and furthered by studying *The 5 C's of Cinematography* by Joseph V. Mascelli. It was a rigorous exercise, but it paid off. Over time, depending on their interest, each brother was assigned an area of expertise by their father. That is how the 'Ramsay Brothers' were born.

My mother, Asha, is Fatechand Uttamchand Ramsay's daughter, sister to the Ramsay Brothers. Their original surname – Ramsinghani – was shortened to the easier-to-pronounce 'Ramsay' for the benefit of their British clientele. After Partition, the family moved to Mumbai from Karachi and my grandfather, F.U. Ramsay, who was a radio engineer, continued dealing in electronics. My mother, then a little girl, would watch him work, soldering the pieces of a Murphy radio together. Sometimes, he would look up and tease her, play-acting like he was going to jab her with the solder. She would shriek in fear. That was a special game between the father and daughter.

The radio business was changing, so F.U. secured an agency from the Binny and Co. brand and began selling fabric. It was a large household to run, with many mouths to feed – Kumar, Kamla, Gangu, Tulsi, Maya (known as Asha after marriage), Arjun, Keshu, Shyam and Karan. There were seven brothers and two sisters. My mother, Asha, is the younger of the two. Then there was Gopal, another Ramsay brother, who was born after Gangu and passed away as a toddler. Sati, too, a sister born prior to Asha died within a week of birth.

Like many small businessmen in those days, my grandfather was drawn to the film industry and wanted to make movies. The fervour of Partition was still in the air, which led to the patriotic *Shahid-E-Azam Bhagat Singh* in 1954. This was followed by *Rustom Sohrab* in 1963, the result of Kumar Ramsay's fascination with the classic Persian legend. Both films clicked at the box office.

The 1970 film *Ek Nanhi Munni Ladki Thi* became the turning point in the Ramsay's filmmaking business. While the movie did not do well, both Shyam and Tulsi noticed the audience's positive reaction to the scene where Prithviraj Kapoor wore a scary mask. It was clear that being scared was a thrill for the audience. Based on this, the two brothers convinced their father to make a horror film. F.U. was ready to give up on the risky business of films but he gave in to the enthusiasm of his sons and supported their idea. Each one of them was trained in an aspect of filmmaking, making them a formidable and self-reliant unit.

The first attempt of the brothers was a Sindhi film called *Naqli Shaan*. A year later, in 1972, they made *Do Gaz Zameen Ke Neeche*, the production that finally steered them to their destined genre of horror.

The rest is history.

I am often asked, 'What was it like to be a grandchild of the Ramsays, where horror was my playground?'

My mother used to take us to visit my Naana and Naani (grandparents) on Saturdays. My maamas, maamis (maternal uncles and aunts) and cousins lived together at Lamington Road in Bombay. My grandparents would be sitting on their individual beds, which were joined at the head in the narrow room. On seeing me, my grandmother would delightedly greet me with her characteristic hearty laugh and draw me into a warm hug. Then she would untie the knot at the end of her sari to give me some money from her hidden stash. I would bashfully refuse, even though I secretly wanted to grab the notes. She would then squeeze the money in my eager palm. Later, I would jump onto my grandfather's bed. He would ruffle my hair, planting an affectionate kiss on my cheek. As I grew older, the kiss was replaced by a gentle hug.

With the money my grandmother had given me, I would buy a variety of sweets and wrap a mixture of them in paper. Along with my cousin sister, who was my partner in crime, we would run down to the office and sell our version of 'paan' to my indulgent uncles for one rupee a packet. They would look up smiling from their animated discussions and rummage for change in their pockets. At the end, I always made a profit and went home with double the money. This was my ritual for years on end.

Another memory I have of those days is being assigned the task of tearing open envelopes in the buzzing office at Lamington Road and arranging the contents neatly. The envelopes contained photographs and letters from aspiring actors and actresses wanting to be cast in a Ramsay film. My cousins and I would enjoy discussing the merits and demerits of the aspirants and their entreating requests. Most of them were from small towns, looking for their big break in Bollywood – youthful men with Rajesh Khanna-like haircuts striking a pose; young women wearing skimpy dresses, looking seductively at the camera in the hope of being a heroine or perhaps even a cadaver in the next Ramsay movie. It was a tad pitiful, because even to our immature minds, most of them would not make the cut. The elusive dreams of stardom were flippantly strewn across that desk.

There was a portion of the office, which was always fascinating to me. It was the Ramsays' dark room, with trays in which negatives from films under production would be developed and the photos hung to dry. It was like a secret room away from the chatter of the outer office. The red lighting cast a surreal glow on the black-and-white stills of menacing monsters and their hapless victims. I would inevitably make my way there and bravely pore over each photograph, each scarier than the last. Alone, I could barely spend a few minutes there before darting back to the comfort of the soothing daylight and my uncles' avid discussions of the ongoing or upcoming productions.

Actors and actresses would come in for their story sittings. Technicians, music directors and whomsoever was involved with the films frequented the office. Plates of boiled eggs garnished with salt and pepper were offered to visitors and a grated apple milk drink or watermelon juice served as the thirst quencher. These were in uninterrupted supply because the vendors ran their business at the office doorstep.

There were always some people hanging around outside, trying to catch a glimpse of the action taking place inside. I felt very privileged that I could walk in and out as I pleased and not be stuck in the sweltering heat like the curious bystanders were. As soon as I opened the office door, jostling onlookers would attempt to peek inside the mystery that was the Ramsays.

Casually lying around were terrifying masks of ghouls, monsters and witches. I still remember the smell of the latex rubber as I tried them on and scampered around the office trying to spook everyone and being a pest. The one thing I can say about my maternal family is that they were unfailingly kind and gentle, amused at my antics. Finally, exhausted and hungry, I would make my way up the stairs to the family residence, where my grandmother waited with a big smothering hug, a paper dosa and sheera from the neighbouring Ramanjaneya restaurant.

I also went for a couple of location shoots and saw the Ramsay monsters upfront, but I would barely bat an eyelid. Watching an actor turn into a fiend from scratch was not particularly frightening.

When the film was ready, the Ramsay clan got to see it in all its gory finality. The same monsters, who were not so fearsome during the shoot, were so petrifying that I would have nightmares for days on end. That was the high! That hair-raising moment where you don't want to look at the screen, but you can't look away either.

The intoxicating rush of terror stayed with us, and so my mother and I devoured horror films over the years. That was our link to each other and to her family. In the course of our binge-watching, my mother and I suggested that her brothers watch a suspense film we had enjoyed. They did, and the story captured their imagination. An adaption followed – *Telephone*, one of the rare Ramsay Brothers murder mystery movies.

Regretfully, like my childhood, it all ended.

My grandparents passed away. Their beds touching each other lay empty. The brothers ultimately went their separate ways. The overgrown sisal tree that my grandfather had planted now covers the naked desolation of the building at Lamington Road. Their films released and faded into oblivion. The office remains locked with the eroded Ramsay Films banner holding on to the past. That era of horror is over, and only the memories and movies remain.

My mother, Asha, whom my father affectionately calls 'horror sister', missed her calling.

While narrating her supernatural experiences for this book, she would excitedly add dramatic elements of horror: 'Why don't you say that her nails were dripping blood?' or 'Her eyeballs turned upwards!' I would have to keep reminding her that I was writing true accounts of the experiences, not a Ramsay script. Even though she understood that the book is about staying authentic, old habits die hard. I had to be a strict taskmaster to keep her narratives from straying into fiction.

But in these moments, it struck me that horror was in my mother's genes. She could create such scenes with a snap of her finger. Her eyes would shine as her imagination soared into the universe of horror.

I credit my creativity to my maternal family, predominantly my mother – the original storyteller. The ability to create a world with words is my inheritance. Destiny has driven me from birth along many pit-stops to halt at the eventual destination of this book.

I was born at the precise moment my father was speeding past the Chandanwadi crematorium in South Mumbai, trying to get my mother to the hospital in time. It was just over an hour past midnight when he jammed the brakes of his Ambassador car, BMC 9931, on hearing my new-born cries emanating from the backseat, as I lay cradled in the folds of my paternal grandmother's saree.

And so, the final resting place of people became my birthplace. While some are to the manor born, I was to the spirits born.

The Family Tree of Horror

Fatechand U. Ramsay *m* Kishni (Motial)

*Kumar *m* Sheela

| Gopal | Raj | Sunil |

*Kamla *m* Gurdas Katara

| Anil | Prem |

*Gangu *m* Veena

| Chander | Geeta |

*Tulsi *m* Kanta

| Pramila | Pushpa | Deepak |

*Maya (Asha) *m* Devidas Thawani

| Priti | Harish | Jaya |

Priti (Alisha) *m* Johnny Kirpalani

| Sascha | Tiana |

*Arjun *m* Rajkumari (Kavita)

| Tanuja | Dharam | Amit |

*Keshu *m* Kavita

| Dinesh | Mayur (Aryeman) | Sagar |

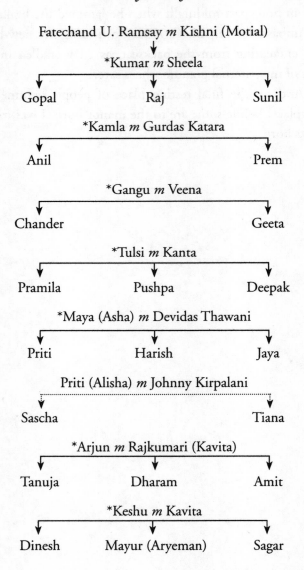

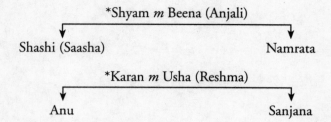

*Shyam *m* Beena (Anjali)

Shashi (Saasha)   Namrata

*Karan *m* Usha (Reshma)

Anu   Sanjana

* The children of F.U. Ramsay

In Sindhi culture, women also change their first name along with their surname after marriage. Name changes post-marriage are in brackets.

Freeze

They freeze sometimes, the dead.
Straddled between two worlds, the path, unclear.
Trapped and full of doubt and fear.
Trying to get into your head.

The Lamp

The seven brothers were better known as the Ramsay Brothers, called thus by their producer father, F.U. Ramsay. The two sisters, Asha and Kamla, have rarely been mentioned in celluloid history. This is the tale of the younger sister, Maya, better known as Asha after marriage. Only five of the brothers – Gangu, Tulsi, Arjun, Keshu, Shyam – and both the sisters were present at the time of this incident, which occurred around sixty years ago. Kumar, the eldest, had stayed back in Mumbai to look after the business; Karan, the youngest, was not yet born.

Holidays mean all play and no work for children, and it was no different for the Ramsay kids. This particular vacation was even more special – it was going to be spent in Ajmer at the house of their maternal aunt, whom the children affectionately called 'Dadi'. She lived in a large but modest flat on the second floor of an old three-storey building, meagre in its trimmings. It was a typical structure of an era when high rises were a futuristic dream and elevators almost non-existent.

Back then, life was simple, both in its pleasures and its offerings – no television, no mobile phones, no computers, no video games. Time spent with family was treasured. Getting fresh air and playing games outdoors was an integral part of the day.

Upon their arrival in Ajmer, F.U. Ramsay, the patriarch, and his wife, Motial, were received with delight by the latter's widowed sister. Dadi had lost her husband in childhood and had since lived with a friend who, too, had been widowed young. With no children of her own, Dadi was always amused and intrigued by the crazy chatter of her sister's brood. The children ran all over the place, their excitement over the new surroundings shooting adrenalin through their veins. The elders tried to catch up with each other but could hardly hear themselves talk amidst the din in the house.

After they had finished settling into their respective shared bedrooms, the children went to the living room scrounging for food. They stuffed themselves with the snacks lying on the table. The sugar rush, an aftermath of bingeing on sweet biscuits, made them even more fidgety.

'Can we go down and play?' asked Gangu.

'Please, please, Dada, can we?' beseeched Tulsi.

Asha, who was closest in age to Tulsi, stuck like glue to him and looked at her parents expectantly.

Their father looked at his wristwatch. It was almost 6 p.m. 'I want you home soon!' he ordered.

'Children, please don't stop at the first floor. Go down straight and be home before sunset. Promise?' urged Dadi.

The kids squealed in delight as they put on their shoes and unanimously promised to return in time. Asha, always the curious one, asked, 'Why can't we stay later and why shouldn't we stop at the first floor?'

'Because Dadi said so!' replied Motial, even though she knew that the answer was not going to satisfy her inquisitive daughter.

Dadi came to the rescue. 'Nobody has lived there for a long while, child. So that house is very dirty. You don't want to fall ill going near a dirty house, do you?'

Asha had more questions, but Tulsi dragged her away, and they went bounding down the stairs.

The deathly silence of the first floor was in stark contrast to the obvious signs of life in the floors above. The flat had a grilled window and an ancient padlocked door. Rust and cobwebs hung from both. Staleness hung in the air. And despite it being broad daylight, it was unnaturally dark. The older children felt a sense of foreboding, while the distracted younger ones were mostly oblivious. Tulsi stood at the bottom of the stairs and shouted out his own name. His voice came vibrating back in an angry echo. The children scampered away, scared out of their wits.

They spent an enjoyable evening playing with other kids who lived in the building. When the sun had almost set, they marched back home obediently. They passed the first floor, and those who dared to sneak a glance realized that there was a dim light emanating from the brooding window of the padlocked flat. Nobody wanted to venture into the palpable eeriness of the place, especially after all that they had learned about the strange house from their new playmates. Kamla and Arjun were the most petrified. Narrowing their eyes into tiny slits, they ran up the stairs at breakneck speed. The others showed more bravado, but there was a quickness to all their footsteps.

'You said nobody lives there, then how come there is a light in the window?' Asha asked Dadi as soon she ran into the house.

'Somebody in the building must have lit the lamp. I don't really know, child. Such a small girl and so many big questions!'

'Because there is a ghost there! Of a woman. She is the one who lights the lamp at sunset every day. That's why nobody stays there because of the ghost, Dadi,' Gangu announced proudly. He had been informed by the other children who had told the newcomers about the house on the first floor.

'I have stayed here for so many years. You think I would not know about a ghost, if there was one? Those children are pulling your leg. It is an empty house, and nobody has lived there for as long as I can remember,' Dadi insisted, trying desperately to find a way to divert attention from the house.

Looking at their curious faces, their mother chimed in, 'Good children who pray to God don't ever have to worry about ghosts.'

And that was that.

The Ramsay children went down to play daily, leaping over the distance between the first floor and the ground floor, two to three steps at once. Their hearts always hammered wildly before the descent from Dadi's home to the ground floor. But it was a risk they had to take to make the most of their invaluable playtime. The corroded window was inescapable, so they walked in single file on the farthest side of the staircase. They tried to be home before it turned dark, but on occasion, when they would forget to get back in time, the lamp would inevitably be burning – like a sword hanging over their heads. The later in the evening it got, the brighter the flame burnt.

Fear was a great deterrent to flouting the rules. Kamla always prayed on her way up and down the stairs. The very young children clung on to her tightly. Arjun would reflexively turn his face to the other side. The only act of daring the remaining siblings permitted themselves was to yell their own names from the ground-level stairs. The stillness spat out that monstrous snarl of an echo, which only resounded from the first floor – no other floor, no matter the permutations and combinations they tried.

Perhaps it was the incident with her elder sister, Kamla, always very timid, that pushed Asha's eight-year-old mind into rebellion. Since the day they had entered Dadi's house, Kamla had hated being alone and constantly looked over her shoulder as though she could sense someone ... or something. One day, she was bathing in the bathroom attached to her room. She quickly finished her shower and dried herself. But when she tried to open the bathroom door, Kamla was hauled back inside. Her bones turned to liquid when she swivelled her head. Latching on to her shoulder was an arm. It had mangled fingers with muddy corkscrew nails that were digging into her skin. The grisly arm was suspended mid-air and stretched across the bathroom.

Kamla ran out of the bathroom screaming. On hearing her screams, her parents came hurtling inside. Kamla was shaking like a leaf. Kishni grabbed hold of her distressed daughter.

'What happened? What happened?' asked a worried F.U. Ramsay.

'I don't want to stay here! I want to go home. Someone ... something tried to catch me in the bathroom. It was only an arm and it was this long!' Kamla was incoherent and hysterical, as she revealed the welts on her shoulder. 'See ... I have these marks too. It grabbed me. I escaped. I don't want to stay in Dadi's house here. That arm ...'

'How can there be an arm without a person's body? Those children in the building have scared all of you with their ghost stories. You must have hurt yourself in the shower or scraped the towel hooks without realizing it,' her father tried to reason with a traumatized Kamla.

'I would know if I had hurt myself! I know what happened. There is a ghost in that house and also in this house! Who puts on the lamp every night? How can it light itself? I am telling you I saw the arm! It was detached and hanging in the air. Please, please, take me home!'

'There is no such thing as ghosts! Like Dadi told you, some neighbour must be lighting the lamp. Dadi will feel very bad if we leave like this, only because you have had a bit of a fright. Now calm down, or your brothers and sisters will get scared and start believing in this nonsense, too.'

There was no point in arguing with her father. Kamla had no option except to toe the line for everyone's sake.

That evening, after sunset, Asha did not follow the others home but defiantly walked towards the diffused glow of the first floor. She wanted to prove to herself and the others that there was nothing to fear, so that they could enjoy the remainder of their holiday. But as the ominous glow from the house snaked towards her, Asha's resolve to find out what lay behind the locked door started to falter. But to her brave eight-year-old mind, there was neither retreat nor surrender at this point. Her hands were shaking as she tried to pry open the window through the rusted grills, frantically dusting off the cobwebs and dirt that stuck to her skin.

The glass, caked with ages of neglect, allowed no visibility. Asha pushed harder, and with a groan it opened slightly. Her heart was in her mouth and a sickly feeling ran through her. A putrid smell of decay assaulted her nostrils. The first thing Asha saw through the slit was the earthen lamp, its wick lit, and the flickering incandescence draping the wall and sweeping the floor. Her eyes grew wide in horror at the sight before her.

There was no floor. The entire base of the room was a series of bars, like those of a prison. The leaping shadows cast by the flame seemed to take on a life of their own. It was as if the room was breathing, pulsating. Asha was mesmerized and terrified at the same time. Curiosity fuelled her courage as she pressed her face to the glass trying to peep way down inside to see what was beneath those bars, but the window grill blocked her view.

Who had lit the lamp?

Though Asha could not see anybody, her senses warned her that there was somebody in that room.

Suddenly, just beneath those grills, there was movement.

Asha jumped out of her skin!

It was a flash of a woman's fleeting form, which disappeared almost as soon as it had appeared.

Asha's heart was thudding wildly as survival instinct cautioned her to run back upstairs. But now that she had seen what she perceived to be a person, she had to find out the truth at any cost.

Who was in that room?

A resolute Asha used all her strength to push the window in a bit further, as far as her arm could go. The tarnished metal budged ever so slightly.

The freezing cold air inside engulfed her sweat-drenched body, sending a shiver down her spine. The lamp flickered in a frenzy as a giant shadow enveloped the room, looming larger and larger before her eyes.

There she was!

Asha lost her balance, but she could not peel her eyes away from the terrifying sight in front of her. It was a woman with mercury-silver hair. She was inkier than her own shadow. The woman was pacing back and forth. Her rotting nails, caked with layers of dirt, stroked the bars that entrapped her in this hellish house. Suddenly, without any warning, Asha felt a sharp, piercing pain slicing her arm. Horror-struck, she yanked it back and scrambled up the stairs, into Dadi's house and straight to the sanctuary of her room.

Asha's brother, Tulsi, saw her rushing in and trailed her. 'What took you so long?' he asked. At first, Asha was incomprehensible and pale as a ghost. Tulsi held his trembling sister's hand as they both stared transfixed at the deep, angry fingernail scratches running across her frail arm. They were similar to the ones on Kamla's arm and just as inexplicable, as were the spine-chilling sightings that both sisters had had.

The family went home a few days later. The children, who never went back there, were especially relieved to leave Ajmer behind. But more than six decades later, the haunting memories of Ajmer have never quite left them.

As a young adult, Asha Thawani (née Maya Ramsay) narrated a story idea loosely-based on a film she had seen, to her father, F.U. Ramsay. The story became the Ramsays' foray into horror – *Do Gaz Zameen Ke Neeche* and Indian cinema's first full-fledged horror film. Kumar Ramsay masterfully fleshed out the story and wrote the script, setting a new benchmark in Indian horror. The already married and shy, young Asha never took credit for her role in the making of the film. Many years thereafter, she hesitatingly recollected the real-life events of Ajmer to her daughter, Alisha 'Priti' Kirpalani. Unintentionally, the seed for this book was sown back then. Little did her daughter know that this was just the beginning.

Resting Place

At last she hoped to rest,
having passed through life's test.
For heaven she still waits,
lingering outside its hallowed gates.

The Hitchhiker

The soft-spoken late Shyam Ramsay was the sixth of the Ramsay Brothers and at the helm of many a successful Ramsay horror film. He was addicted to his craft and was in a non-stop process of experimentation with the horror genre – be it. The Zee Horror Show *on television or a new-age horror web series.*

The year was 1983. After wrapping up the gruelling production of *Purana Mandir*, Shyam Ramsay decided to stay back and unwind in Mahabaleshwar. Mahabaleshwar has been the location for many Ramsay films. It is also a town where a number of family members experienced the unfathomable. The Ramsay clan spent a fair amount of time at the hill station while shooting or holidaying.

After a few days of rest and recuperation, it was time to return home to Bombay. Shyam was looking forward to the drive ahead. The lonely road – hardly any man or vehicle on the way – was a treat, and something he looked forward to. If there is one thing the family members had in common besides the love for all things horror, it was their love for long drives.

So, that night, Shyam took off from Mahabaleshwar. He picked night-time because it would be faster, barely anyone on the road, and he could beat the traffic when he reached Bombay. He knew the area like the back of his hand and drove through the winding roads with full expertise. The headlights of the occasional passing trucks and cars blinked rapidly at him as he stepped on the accelerator. The speeding tyres devoured kilometre after kilometre, until he slowed down in anticipation of the road ahead.

There were no streetlights on the upcoming sweep of the deserted highway. As he drove cautiously in that poor visibility, he spotted the unmistakable silhouette to the right side of the road. The person was bathed in moonlight, a striking contrast to the darkness around.

A lady? At this hour?

The woman's right thumb was upright, requesting a ride. She paced a bit and stood still, arm extended, trying to flag the car down.

No woman in her right mind would be standing here alone this late in the night. She must be in some sort of trouble.

In two minds whether to stop or not, the gentleman in Shyam won and he slowed down. As he pulled up, he asked, 'Hello, all well?'

The woman looked at him blankly and then jerkily crossed the road and moved towards the passenger side of the car. Startled by her unpredictable move, Shyam stuck his head further out of the rolled down window. It was a hot and humid night.

'Where are you going? I am headed to Bombay. Can I drop you along the way?' he asked.

Without any acknowledgement of having heard him, the woman got into the car. A waft of cold air came in with her and shrouded him with its frosty discomfort.

What is with the weather today? Unbearably hot to unbearably cold in seconds?

Shyam's stomach was starting to feel queasy. Rubbing his palms together, he held out his hand. 'Hi, I am Shyam.'

Not a word. She did not even respond to his handshake and kept staring blankly ahead.

'And … you are?'

Still not a word.

What a strange woman! Perhaps she was hearing-impaired?

She was beautiful, though. Peculiar, but undeniably beautiful. Her dishevelled hair was jet black, reaching her waist and framing her alabaster face. She wore a simple white sari, and her hands were tucked in the warmth of its folds. But it was her eyes that struck Shyam the most. Eyes were supposed to be the windows to the soul. Hers were lifeless – not a flicker of expression in them.

Shyam attempted some small talk as she watched him vacantly. Like a crashing wave trying to reach the shore, with what seemed to be considerable effort, the lady in white finally tried to say something. The utterance was as gritty as sandpaper, like there was something stuck in her throat. It was more a rumble than a voice and altogether incoherent. Shyam had never heard anything like it, and it grated on his nerves. He wanted to shut his ears to drown out the harsh screech.

Why did I give her a lift and get myself into this mess? She is ruining my relaxing drive back home.

There was something very unsettling about the woman. Shyam abandoned the thought of carrying on a conversation with her, and they drove on in silence. As the journey continued, his sense of unease grew – a distinct feeling that something was wrong. The car was filled with the smell of fetid air. Though the temperature had dropped a few degrees since the woman sat in his car, Shyam felt hot and sweaty, his palms clammy. He lowered the temperature of the air-conditioner and stole a sideways look at the lady to see if she seemed as uncomfortable as him.

Her face was like chiselled stone, and there was a diffused glow around her head, which highlighted her fragile skin. There was something creepy about this woman. He could not put his finger on it, but he knew he wanted to drop her off at the nearest viable point.

'Do let me know where you need to get off,' he said politely. His voice did not betray the slightest trace of his inner turmoil.

The woman kept looking straight ahead, as if in some sort of trance.

How long am I going to be stuck with her?

With a sigh of resignation, Shyam let his eyes wander over his unsettling passenger. When they settled on her feet, he nearly crashed into the divider. Her feet were turned inwards. The toenails were gnarled and twisted, like those of a wild animal. His heart was pounding as if it would burst out of his chest.

All those stories of witches Shyam had researched for his movies suddenly flooded in his mind.

Is this woman even human?

Now that he scrutinized her, he felt that there was really nothing that suggested that possibility. Her abnormal mannerisms and those distorted feet were damning evidence. As far as he was concerned, he was dealing with an ungodly creature.

Pinpricks of fear pierced through Shyam's skin like glass splinters. Escape plans were racing through his mind, but they all ended disastrously, even in his imagination. By this time, Shyam was totally spooked. He tried to figure out a way to get the woman out of the car as soon as he could, but without antagonizing her or revealing his fear.

But how?

Shyam toyed with several getaway strategies. Should he leave the car and run? Where would he go at this time? How far could he run on this isolated road, with neither help nor hope in sight? There were not many fools like him who would give lifts to strangers. What would his wife and daughters do, if he never returned home? What if the woman sitting beside him could read his mind?

Shyam glanced at his passenger and almost let go of the steering wheel in fright, because she was staring right at him. Her face inches away, head cocked to one side. Her vacuous eyes were endless tunnels of emptiness, and he felt her eyes would suck him right in. He got a shock when he heard her gravelly voice gurgle unintelligibly. It took Shyam a while to register that the woman was pointing towards the road with her lengthy fingers, wagging her talon-like nails.

Is she going to rip out my throat with those razor sharp nails?

Shyam felt beyond stupid. He must have been blind not to have put two and two together, and now he would pay the price for his foolhardiness.

It was pitch dark. The area was desolate. The predatory trees appeared as though they were swooping lower and lower, readying for the kill. Shyam decided not to question the woman and slammed the brakes. The car groaned to a halt.

Is this it? The end?

Shyam shut his eyes and, praying fervently, braced himself for what was going to come next.

The car door opened and without saying another word, the hitchhiker slid out of the car and faded away into the darkness.

A tidal wave of relief flooded through Shyam. *She was gone.* He could not believe how fortunate he had been. He gripped the steering wheel and tried to gather his wits, half expecting her to reappear. He looked cautiously in the direction she had headed, thanking his lucky stars that he was rid of her and had escaped from her clutches.

Was she really a witch or merely a deformed woman? Whatever she was, there was something sinister about her. Who goes into a dense forest at this hour?

Shyam vowed not give a lift to anybody ever again. *Never!* He sat back and savoured the safety of his car's locked windows and doors.

Then, as if in the movies, the clouds cleared and made way for the moon.

Realisation dawned and spasms of fresh fear pumped through Shyam. Nothing could have prepared him for what he saw, as little by little, scattered, shimmering crosses revealed themselves. Shyam was parked right outside a graveyard!

Drive, Shyam, drive, before she comes back again!

Shyam feverishly tried the ignition, but the key kept slipping from his fumbling hands. By and by, the vehicle growled into action, and he made a speedy escape. In an unbelievable and ironic twist, the prolific horror filmmaker had unwittingly dropped off a spirit back to her home, on his way back home.

Inspired by this occurrence, five years later, in 1988, Shyam Ramsay made the film *Veerana*. It was a huge success and is deemed to be one of the Ramsay Brothers' best films. The story was that of a beautiful young girl possessed by the vindictive spirit of a witch, who wandered around desolate places to seduce men and eventually kill them. Luckily for Shyam Ramsay, reel life did not emulate real life, and he lived to tell the tale.

Wandering

I have nowhere to go.
No repose, only my woe.
That world or this?
Life, death, neither is bliss.

The Jogger

Gangu Ramsay, the second son of F.U. Ramsay, was the cinematographer. He captured the nuances of horror films through his camera lens. Perhaps that is what gave him the sensitivity of observation to see things that surpassed the tangible.

A host of Ramsay films such as *Hotel, Guesthouse* and *Dak Bangla* were shot at Hotel Anarkali in Mahabaleshwar. The hill station's proximity to Mumbai made it the ideal destination and a staple feature in Ramsay movies. It was a matter of logistics. The closer the destination, the more economical the budget for the film. Moreover, the hill station had isolated lanes, quiet graveyards and deep forests – the perfect backdrop to create an atmosphere of horror.

Apart from Hotel Anarkali, the Ramsays also made use of a government guesthouse as a production set. These two places were where the crew camped and the Ramsays vacationed.

The extended duration of time that goes into shooting movies meant that for weeks on end, family members would be on location together, regardless of their level of involvement with the production. Everyone pitched into the family business. The wives helped with cooking and make-up and the children enjoyed the holiday, happy to run errands that came their way. The films were jokingly called 'tiffin-box productions', a term coined by F.U. Ramsay himself.

It was one whopping picnic, with ghost stories thrown in, ideas rallying back and forth and, on occasion, even unexpectedly digging up a hidden grave while installing the sets. Accidentally unearthing skeletons was an occupational hazard and all in a day's work for the Ramsay brood.

Since horror is most effectively portrayed in the dark, a major portion of shoot took place in the late hours of the night.

After wrapping up the production for the day, the family would often stroll back to the hotel. This gave them an opportunity to enjoy the cool weather as well as brainstorm for the next stage of shooting. However, even for seasoned horror aficionados, the darkness brought with it a feeling of eeriness, so there was an unsaid understanding that they would always travel in groups at night.

Gangu and his wife, Veena, were also on location in Mahabaleshwar. Even though the family usually stayed at Hotel Anarkali or the government guesthouse, this time, Gangu and Veena were staying at another hotel.

In the wake of pack-up being announced earlier than usual, the two of them decided to have dinner at a restaurant before heading back to the hotel. Along with a few other unit members, the couple chose to walk. It was the perfect way to walk off the after-effects of a generous meal.

As the road was uneven and poorly lit, the group trooped in a single file, keeping an eye out for snakes or any other nocturnal animal that might cross their path. The sounds of nature at night were amplified, which made the journey even more nerve-racking, especially after a gruelling shoot.

The operatic crickets were at their shrillest best. The stillness of the night was punctured periodically by the shrieking of bats hanging upside down from trees or flitting in the sky, or a mischievous monkey waking from his slumber and letting out a sudden cry. Each sound sent shivers of alarm down the spine. A flutter here, a rustle there – all of it added to the unnerving mood, disturbing the tranquillity of the walk.

The air was nippy. Sauntering along, each one in the group soaked in the mystery of the night, some picking up pace, eager to find their beds. Veena and Gangu were trailing at the rear.

After chattering for a bit, a quiet descended on the group. The noisy night suddenly turned as silent as the jagged stones around them. Not one cricket could be heard, nor a bat flapping anymore. The forest and its inhabitants had turned mysteriously mute. A gust of frigid air surrounded Gangu and Veena.

It was Veena who saw it first. Her hair stood on end as she realized that there was something beside her, matching its pace to the couple's stride, quickening its steps to fall in line with them.

Having spent months of her married life on a Ramsay movie set, in proximity to all things unnatural, a primal sensibility of self-preservation warned her to look straight ahead. Her heart lurched in panic, and she stumbled while hastening to move closer to her husband. Once close to Gangu, she looked back furtively from the corner of her eyes. What she saw was enough to turn her legs into jelly.

Oh my God!

She clasped her husband's shoulder, as words froze in her mouth.

Gangu had already seen the apparition by their side but had chosen to keep quiet, not wanting to scare his wife. At first, he had thought someone from the unit was wearing a mask, trying to frighten them. Then he had got a better look. His eyes met Veena's in mutual terror.

Please, please this cannot be happening. What are you? Who are you?

The apparition was male, but not exactly a man. It was the head of a man. In the dark, it glowed yellow. It was round, abnormally round, emitting a pasty, jaundiced pallor. The face was bloated like a full moon, and there were no distinguishable features – no a nose or a mouth. Though the features were smudged, it had definitely been human once. There was no discernible body below the face, and yet, the disembodied creature was walking as if by magic.

Bob. Bob. Bob.

Bobbing like a playful devil's balloon, up and down the head went matching the sloping terrain on the narrow path.

Gangu's first reaction was for the couple to make a run for it. But he realized that it would be futile, given the ease with which the visage kept pace with them, matching every stride.

If this had been a thief, Gangu would have put up a fight. But how does one contend with something otherworldly?

An agitated Veena, meanwhile, goaded him to keep moving faster. *Run!*

The duo picked up speed, walking as fast as their feet could carry them.

The head floated alongside, turning blurry, as though running right with them.

Bounce. Bounce. Bounce.

As the duo slowed down, hoping it would pass them by, it too became slower.

Flop. Flop. Flop.

The march from hell continued in a perfect tandem of unmitigated terror. The ghoul was glued to them. To Gangu and Veena, it seemed as if the living, throbbing forest was tongue-tied and the only sound permeating the habitat was the effort of their ragged breathing. Gangu's palms were sweating as he held his wife's quivering hands tightly. He wanted to shout out to their companions, who were ahead of them. But he realized that they were too far away from them to be able to hear him.

Keep quiet. Do not run but do not slow down. Act cool. Act calm. Breathe. Breathe. Breathe.

Gangu did not want to trigger any hostility in the spirit. He hoped his legs would not give way because he did not want the creature to catch him immobilized. So far, the phantom had not harmed them and – God willing – if they got lucky, it would go away on its own.

Om. Om. Om.

Chanting mantras as he tried to focus on moving swiftly, rather than concentrate on their ghostly company, Gangu continued to hold his wife as they made their way along the path. As leaves squelched beneath their feet, a similar sound echoed beside them.

Squelch. Bob.

Squelch. Flop.

Squelch. Bounce.

Om. Om. Om.

Each step was peppered with the litany of the chant now.

The hotel was a stone's throw away. Gangu could no longer see the rest of the group. They must have headed to their rooms, assuming the duo was enjoying a romantic midnight walk.

Damn it!

He stole a rapid glance to see if the spectre was still with them. Sure enough!

Bob. Bob. Flop. Flop. Bounce. Bounce.

Like a slowly spinning globe on an invisible axis, it was right beside them, as if it were the most natural thing in the world – his featureless face, grotesque, moving in an unfaltering, gliding motion.

The gates of the hotel were in view by now. They could see the dimly-lit nameplate. Gangu felt relief engulfing him. But the nearer it got, the further it seemed. Just a few seconds longer, and hopefully, they would be safe.

Determined to make it to the refuge of the hotel, dragging Veena with him, Gangu began to run faster than he ever had.

They ran. The spirit ran. The distance between them remained the same – not a centimetre more or less.

Both Gangu and Veena felt as if their lungs would burst, but the spirit showed no indication of slowing down.

The rubble, stones and fallen branches on the unfinished path resonated like bullets as they crushed them underfoot.

Almost there.

Gangu shut his eyes and pulled Veena by the arm as they crossed the iron gates of the hotel. Taking a deep breath, he opened his eyes and looked around.

The spirit had vanished. It had evaporated into nothingness.

Veena was panting heavily. Gangu warily looked around once more. It really was just the two of them. There was no sight or sound of anything else, except the distant barking of a dog and faint sounds of the night. Wherever the apparition had come from, it had withdrawn.

Not wanting to push their luck, Gangu and Veena scurried as fast at their unsteady legs could carry them, till they reached the sanctum of their room. Hands shaking, Gangu locked the door firmly behind them.

Lying in bed, neither spoke, still trembling at their blood-curdling encounter. The moonlight cascaded into the room, covering their inert forms. For the rest of their lives, the sallow colour of the moon remained a grim reminder of that night and their close shave with the supernatural.

Gangu has filmed monsters all his life, but the image of that beheaded entity stays permanently imprinted in his mind.

The incident occurred a long time ago. While time and age dulled the memory of that fateful night, Gangu Ramsay went on to experience more than his fair share of supernatural encounters. Once while driving back from Lonavala, past the Bushi Dam, he noticed an alluringly beautiful woman. She was perched on a boulder. He blinked twice to make sure he was not imagining her, but his wife had seen her, too. There she was, a celestial beauty unlike any other. He drove past, mystified, but could not resist looking back at her through the rear-view mirror. But she had vanished into thin air.

In recent years, both Gangu and Veena have begun sensing a presence in their house. Veena finds a tapping on her arm or her leg while she is asleep, even though her husband is on the other side of the bed. Gangu wakes up intermittently through the night to see the silhouette of a woman standing near the dresser or the window. At times, he feels her touch even though the bed is empty. Gangu and Veena live alone but never feel alone, because along with the moon, someone always seems to be watching.

A Mother's Love

I was but a child,
wrenched from my mother's embrace.
I look at her wrinkled face,
her hair unkempt and wild.
I was but a child.

The Favourite

The late Keshu Ramsay was the flamboyant one among the siblings. He piped a different tune from the rest of the Ramsay Brothers. He broke away from the family, much to the disappointment of his father, F.U. Ramsay. He is best known for his hit 'Khiladi' series and close to a dozen films with Akshay Kumar, who thereafter reached the dizzying heights of superstardom. Once Keshu found Akshay, whom he considered a fourth son, he wanted to work with him in every film.

A mother's love is legendary in its boundlessness and she has a treasure trove of it to share among her children. However, sometimes there is a special soul connection with a child, and Motial Ramsay shared such a bond with her fifth son, Keshu. Her children teased her about her favourite child and as much as she denied it, her soft spot was plain for everyone to see. Keshu loved his mother in equal measure. Even in adulthood, he had that naughty twinkle in his eyes which made him so endearing. Though Keshu was fiercely protective of his family, his independent and adventurous personality became the cause for many altercations between father and son.

Motial was an extremely devoted wife to F.U. Ramsay and an equally devoted mother. It broke her heart to witness the fights between Keshu and F.U. While Keshu had a vision of the movies he wanted to make and was the most ambitious of the Ramsay brothers, his father believed that the family should stay together, professionally. Ultimately, Keshu left in pursuit of his dreams, leaving behind the 'Ramsay Brothers' tag. It was hard labour on every front, but he did not give up. In 1986, he released his first film, *Avinash*, under his banner of 'Kishni Films', named after his mother's maiden name. Taking up his father's challenge, he refused to piggyback on the Ramsay name that had been his identity thus far. The movie credits simply flaunted his first name, 'Keshu'.

Through all this, the mother and son kept in constant touch. Every night, Motial would call Keshu to chat with him and his wife, Kavita.

That night in 1982 was no different.

Keshu and Kavita were relaxing in their bedroom after dinner and the telephonic chat. Being night owls, they were lounging in bed, when suddenly, Keshu sat up and exclaimed,

'Let's go to Poona right now. You can ask your brother and his wife to join us.'

'What? At this time? Are you joking? The kids are fast asleep, and I am tired! What is the rush to go now?'

'I am not joking. Let's pack up and leave immediately.'

Judging by his expression, Keshu was most definitely serious.

'It's almost 2 a.m. Why don't we go in the morning? It's not safe to drive at this hour.'

'We can go by taxi. Get the children ready. Don't argue.'

Kavita knew that it was pointless to argue with Keshu once his mind was made up, so she got the children ready. Her sister-in-law said they would follow the next morning. They reached Poona in a few hours and searched for accommodation, but no hotels were available. In the end, they headed to the Boat Club, where they were affiliate members.

While trying to check-in, the receptionist informed them that there was an urgent call from Bombay and that they were to call back. Apparently, messages had been left with some other hotels and clubs in the area as well, in the eventuality that Keshu would check in there.

Keshu dismissed the message, assuming that it was Kavita's sister-in-law getting in touch to find out where they were staying. Kavita, however, did not want to take the message lightly, since it said it was urgent. She insisted on calling back her brother's residence.

Kavita's father answered the phone and asked to speak to Keshu. Keshu's face was inscrutable as he listened to the voice at the other end and then put down the receiver.

'Let's return to Bombay,' Keshu had said grimly.

Kavita was totally perplexed. 'What? We just got here! What is going on with you today? Has something happened?'

In the taxi, Keshu said that his mother was not well, so they were heading back. He sat in the front seat, barely exchanging a word with his wife. When they reached Bombay, they headed straight to the Lamington Road residence.

To his wife, Keshu had simply said, 'Go straight home and change, Kavita. Wear white.'

His voice was controlled. White, the colour of mourning, as stark as the grief it symbolizes. Kavita broke down completely as the earth-shattering meaning of his words sank in.

Death had taken its honed axe and destroyed Keshu's roots, shaken the foundation of his existence. On the phone, he had received the tragic news that his mother was no more. She was only in her early sixties, but a heart attack had dealt a lethal blow.

As reality sank in, Keshu felt like the earth had shifted and swallowed him whole as he plummeted into a free-falling vortex. Who would call him every night asking if he had eaten? Who would ask him how his day went, in the way only his mother would? He would never hear her voice or see her face.

Never. Ever.

What he would give to see her alive and breathing just once more – to feel her soul-warming hug, to hear that full-throated laughter.

The next few hours passed in a state of stupor. Bitterness. Rage. Helplessness. Spurts of emotion. *I should have spent more time with her. If only I had known that the end was so close. She was such a simple and kind-hearted person, why take her away so soon?* Regret. Remorse.

Keshu did not even get to see his mother a last time.

The family had cremated her before he could return.

Keshu always said to his sister Asha that their mother must have wanted to spare him the torment of seeing her lifeless form, a sight that would have haunted him forever. He believed this with utmost certainty.

'I would have died myself if I had seen her body. That's why she must have sent me away.' Perhaps, in her own mysterious way, his mother was trying to spare her favourite son and leave him with the image of his mother as she was in life.

It was the only way he could rationalize the irrational impulse to go to Poona, Motial's passing away while he was on his way there and not reachable, his inability to return in time to see her body reduced to mere ashes. Even in death, his mother had shielded him. Theirs was a link that could not be cut by birth or death, an indestructible bond that tied him to her.

In the hours preceding Motial's death, Gangu, Keshu's elder brother, was in Mahabaleshwar, mixing work with pleasure. In the evenings, he enjoyed roaming around the market. It was a busy place, always bustling with people, as shoppers and shopkeepers thronged the street. In the midst of the crowd, Gangu felt as though he had seen the glimpse of someone familiar. When he looked again, he did a double-take.

How could it be?

The woman was the spitting image of his mother. Shaking his head, he tried getting a better look at her. The lady looked directly at him and smiled. The resemblance to his mother was uncanny. Of course, there was no way his mother could be there, but what an incredible likeness!

Gangu smiled back, feeling a gush of affection for the stranger. Then, in a fraction of a second, she disappeared.

What! Where did she go?

He was stumped and searched for her, but she was nowhere to be seen.

Later that night, Gangu received the devastating phone call informing him of his mother's death. Gangu's anguish was multiplied manifold because he was not by her side at the end. Then, the thought of the lady in the market came to his grieving mind. It all started to make sense then.

It was her – my mother!

She had wanted to say her final goodbye. It had been her spirit that had visited him in that market.

There could be no other explanation.

On the exact same day that Gangu had seen his mother's look-alike in Mahabaleshwar and approximately an hour after Keshu and his family had left for Poona, their mother had passed away in Bombay. A mother's love understands the need of each child. Sometimes it can even breach the boundaries between life and death to reach out, one last time.

The years passed and Keshu made his mark with a series of successful movies. He took his youngest brother, Kiran Ramsay, known in the family as Karan, under his wing and was like a father to him. Motial had entrusted Keshu with the duty of protecting Karan and he kept his word. Karan had also been by Keshu's side through his tough times and the brothers were inseparable.

Keshu always wished that his mother had been around to witness his meteoric rise in the industry. In almost three decades of her passing away, not a day went by when she did not cross his mind. In memory of his mother, Keshu had lovingly positioned a framed photo of her in his house. It made him feel she was still around him.

Keshu had a close relationship with his sisters, who had inherited the mannerisms and looks of their mother.

A few months ahead of his death in 2010, Asha had gone over to spend the day with Keshu at his residence. Asha remembers him asking her if she had noticed that their mother's photograph was turning black. Asha had attributed the change to age or moisture affecting the paper on which it was printed. Both brother and sister had brushed it aside as a natural process of decomposition, hardly paying attention to the fact that the decay was limited to only one spot.

It was only Motial's face that had been mutilated by the black tentacles of mould.

The next time Asha visited her brother's house, their mother's face in the photograph had been utterly destroyed and was indecipherable. Yet, the background remained pristine, untouched by the rot. The rapid deterioration was so selective that the puzzled duo could not find a valid reason for it.

A few months later, Keshu passed away at 1.30 a.m. on 20 October 2010. He was only fifty-nine years old.

On the night of his death, Keshu was in high spirits, dancing with abandon at a party when he collapsed. His zest for life and his big heart had betrayed him. He suffered a fatal heart attack.

The stress of filmmaking is well-documented. The run-around for dates, the non-stop hassles of production and finance, the pressure to keep churning out hits. It is a dangerous cocktail of unadulterated pressure. The film industry is a ruthless place. You are the toast of the town while the going is good. A couple of flops and you risk becoming a has-been.

The indomitable prize-fighter that he was, Keshu had put on his boxing gloves, ready to spar and reclaim that elusive trophy called success that was once his. Nobody in the family realized the lethal ramification of the tension building in him; they could not have imagined that they would lose Keshu at that early an age.

The whole family was shattered by his unanticipated demise, particularly Asha. To this day, she is convinced that the decaying photograph had been an omen of the tragedy to come. She regrets her inability to understand the cues that she believes her deceased mother had been sending. If she had gauged the level of stress her brother was in or the condition of his heart, she might have been able to help him.

Keshu's wife, Kavita, is still devastated by her loss. She laments that she had unwittingly dismissed Keshu's last conversation as whimsy. She relives the fateful day over and over. She had woken up that morning to find a contemplative Keshu. It was almost as if he had been waiting for her to wake up so that he could ask her an atypical question.

'Will you marry me in my next life too?'

Kavita was thrown off balance. This was, in every respect, uncharacteristic of Keshu.

'You want me to suffer you in my next life too?' she joked, but there was not a trace of mischief on his serious face.

'Yes, I will marry you in our next lifetime, too,' she finally replied lovingly.

Teasing him about his question that morning is a regret that Kavita will always carry. How was she to know what was to unfold?

Keshu had called at her design studio around 11.30 a.m. and asked her to come home. Though Kavita was bewildered, she obliged, because he had never made such a request before. He was in bed and asked her to lie down beside him. She found his behaviour very disturbing, since they had woken up barely a few hours ago.

Wide-awake, she lay beside him for an hour or so and then went back to her clients. She had asked her son to keep an eye on his father, who was behaving unlike himself.

There were various aberrant occurrences that day, which seem to suggest that Keshu had a premonition of his death. He had agreed to go for a film party at her brother's house after ages. He always wore black at parties, but that day, he asked for blue instead – and socks to match. He got himself a new haircut and even a manicure and pedicure for the first time in his life. He danced with everyone at the party – his sons, his daughters-in-law. He wanted to stay on longer at the event, which, too, was very surprising. As Kavita tried to get him to leave, Keshu asked her to go bid farewell to the hosts. Her back was to him when she had heard a loud thud.

Keshu had fallen to the floor. They could not revive him. Death had the last dance with Keshu, as life slipped away. He was the first of the Ramsay Brothers to die. The brother who dared to dream big was taken away too soon.

Kavita, who bore the tremendous trauma of watching him go, believes he is still here with them. Not in body, but definitely in spirit.

On a couple of other occasions, when Kavita has found herself distraught, sleeping alone in her bedroom, she has felt someone holding her tight, the way Keshu had done when alive. He makes his presence felt, letting her know he is still around with that trademark robust, loving hug – fiercely protective of her as ever.

Keshu, the true khiladi, was never one to play by the rules. He charted his own course in life, in love and even in death.

Keshu supported his youngest brother, Karan, making him an integral part of his life and cinematic career. They were very close to each other. Karan died just a few years after Keshu. He became ill and passed away abruptly, just like his older sibling. He was the second of the Ramsay Brothers to die. With tears in her eyes, Asha recalls the premature demise of both her baby brothers. 'She could not bear to see his suffering, so my mother called back her favourite child, Keshu. Then, in the same way, not wanting to leave him alone, Keshu called back his favourite brother, Karan.'

Waiting

Light, light, they fight the light.
Waiting, waiting, for the dark night.
If you dare to cross their path,
beware of their everlasting wrath.

The King

The gentle and shy Kamla Katara is the first-born daughter of the Ramsay family. She got married at an early age, but kept close contact with her siblings, particularly the late Shyam Ramsay, whom she had been a mother-figure to in his growing years.

The Ramsays spent a few family holidays in Ajmer, where they had relatives. Ajmer is a rich blend of Hindu, Jain and Islamic culture, which reflects in the architecture of the monuments scattered around the city. Going on long drives, squeezed together in their Studebaker car, was an essential feature of the Ramsay vacations.

Travelling with a horde of children must have been an exhausting process for F.U. Ramsay and his wife.

As was common practice among large families in those days, the older siblings were delegated the responsibilities of the younger ones. Usually, the eldest brother, Kumar, was left in charge of business back home. Being second in line, the eighteen-year-old Kamla was the natural choice to be the babysitter for her younger brothers and sisters.

The siblings would wander around the streets of Ajmer, staying close to their aunt's house. In their exploration of the vicinity, they chanced on a perfect spot to run around and have fun. The fact that it was a mausoleum did not bother them in the least.

Abdullah Khan's Tomb is a graceful structure carved out of white marble. Abdullah Khan, also known as Sayyid Mian, was in the service of Emperor Aurangzeb and was renowned for being his commander during the Siege of Bijapur. His two sons, known as the Sayyid Brothers, built the mausoleum in his memory in 1710 AD. The tomb is constructed atop a raised platform that has four steps leading to it. The four towers that flank the tomb are prime examples of late Mughal architecture. A smaller and simpler marble crypt, belonging to Abdullah Khan's wife, lies across the platform and is arresting despite its simplicity.

The children were thrilled with their find and decided to play a game of 'hide and seek' in their new playground. The weather was perfect. It was sunny, but the air was crisp. Kamla was the 'den'. As she counted to ten, she could hear the elation and excitement of the other kids trying to find places to hide.

It was not a very sizeable area, so Kamla found her siblings soon enough, but as much as she searched, she could not find her five-year-old brother Shyam. She kept shouting his name, but there was no response. She circled the unyielding crypt, searching its nooks and crannies, afraid for her brother but still hopeful of catching him.

But when she searched the crypt for the third time, her hands trying to find a concealed opening where he could be hiding, her mouth went dry. A metallic taste coated her tongue. She felt feverish and wanted to throw up. What would her parents do when they found out that Shyam was missing? They had trusted her to look after the children. She counted that all the others were around as they continued their search for him to no avail.

The tomb had a straightforward layout and to lose him in that space was next to impossible, unless he had left the grounds. The thought of Shyam roaming the crowded streets of Ajmer by himself, or worse, never finding him again, made the Ramsay children ramp up their efforts. Kamla began to cry.

What if we never find him? He was such a sweet-looking boy. Someone must have kidnapped him and kept him for themselves. What if they cut off his legs and made a beggar out of him? If something happened to Shyam, how would she live with herself?

As Kamla's wails became louder, the other children became even more nervous and anxious. Where could their brother have gone? How could they leave without him? How would they face their parents?

'Why are you crying?'

It was Shyam's voice!

Kamla looked up, startled, and saw Shyam emerging from the top of Abdullah Khan's tomb. She could not believe it.

How had he even reached there and managed to stay hidden from them for so long, especially since she had gone in and searched the whole area at least three times?

'Where were you? You stupid boy! You scared all of us!'

Kamla was both relieved and angry and she hugged Shyam tight and pinched him hard as she helped him get off the tomb.

He was ice-cold to the touch, just like the marble below her feet.

All the siblings were jumping around, happy to have found Shyam. Loving the attention, the little boy was full of exuberance. He smugly pointed his podgy finger towards the crypt.

'There. I met the King...'

Kamla looked at him curiously.

The tomb was tightly sealed, and there was no means for anyone to enter it. She looked again to confirm. There was no opening from where Shyam could have entered and hidden in the crypt.

The other children were hanging on to every word Shyam spoke, excited by their brother's mysterious disappearance and adventure.

'Stop lying, Shyamu! I will tell Dada. You will get such a beating, you will remember everything.'

The boy stood his ground. 'I am not lying! The king was so nice. He asked me many questions and told me stories about himself. He told me that I would be a famous man one day. When I become rich like the king, I will lock you in jail for shouting at me!'

Despite her anger, Kamla laughed at her brother's childish threat. But she refused to accept a word he said.

'He was not a king! He worked for a king. See, you don't even know that much. How could you have met him? Now tell me, where were you? Tell me the truth, Shyamu!' Kamla said.

'He was dressed like a king, so I thought he was a king. I went to hide under the sheet that was covering the tomb and then the cover opened by itself. He was lying there. He was very old, but he was not scary. He spoke to me. Then, the cover opened again, and I climbed out of the tomb. I swear I am telling the truth.' Shyam sobbed in frustration.

'Okay, stop crying like a baby. Let's go home.' Kamla held Shyam's tiny body close to her.

He was warm now, but chills were coursing down Kamla's spine.

Though she was in denial, she knew it was likely that he had cropped up from the interior of the tomb, but who would believe her?

For the remainder of the holiday, Kamla made sure that the siblings never went back there to play again. It was much easier to hide the truth than to try and seek it.

Despite time passing by, Kamla recalls this experience clearly – because she has replayed it in her mind so often. She has never found a plausible reason as to where Shyam had disappeared and how he reappeared on top of the tomb, as if he had fallen from the heavens. Shyam Ramsay did become a famous man, like the 'king' had predicted.

The Collapse

Unwilling

A long breath, a deep sigh.
The presence of he who did not want to die.
He envies each breath you take.
While you restfully sleep, he is agonizingly awake.

The Collapse

Amit Ramsay, who works in the media, is the younger son of the late Arjun Ramsay, the editor of most Ramsay films. Their family is the sole offshoot of the Ramsays that still resides in the original family home on Lamington Road.

Back in the day, Lamington Road was the moviegoers' paradise. The lavish Apsara and stylish Minerva were two of the most popular theatres in the area. People thronged to the cinema and 'House Full' boards were a common sight. Poised between the two theatres is a building that housed the office and residence of the Ramsays.

The ground floor was the Ramsay Productions office. Film posters of horror-stricken actors intimidated by macabre villains adorned the walls. A poster of Prithviraj

Kapoor looking every inch a monster in a cape, boots and a scary mask stood out. This still from the movie *Ek Nanhi Munni Ladki Thi*, starring Mumtaz, was a landmark moment marking their foray into horror.

The Ramsay brothers would burn the midnight oil so the lights would be on at the oddest hours. Between story sittings and satanic attires tossed around the office, there was an incessant drone of activity and visitors. Family members inhabited the two floors above.

As the family grew, they moved away to different parts of the city. By around the mid-80s, with Keshu's exit, their joint movie business was done and dusted for the most part. Over time, the Ramsay Brothers slowly but surely moved away from each other in location but continued in mixed partnerships. The board outside the locked office at Lamington Road is the only remnant of those heady days of the original team comprising F.U. Ramsay and his seven sons.

Arjun and his family lived on the top floor of the building. A steep, winding, wooden staircase led to their section of the house, which comprised three bedrooms. The family patriarch, F.U. Ramsay, and his wife originally used one of the bedrooms. A sloping aluminium roof added to the antiquity of the place. It was a place where time stood still, obstinate like the mildew adhering to the empty rooms, the evidence of the building's hustle bustle and past glory barely detectable.

Rewind to 2009.

Amit had had a never-ending day. It was after 8 p.m. when he made his way home. The computer classes had burnt him out, and he just wanted to go to bed the minute he reached. As he entered Lamington Road, he saw that the street had been cordoned off and traffic was being diverted. There was chaos everywhere. Fire engines, ambulances, policemen and people swarmed the streets. A building had collapsed. Rescue operations were on in full swing. The magnitude of this catastrophe had choked the locality with onlookers, volunteers and emergency services personnel.

Amit decided to push his way past the smothering crowd, jogging in a tearing hurry. Nobody was at home. Too tired to get himself a snack, he gulped down a glass of water and flopped into bed. His living space was very functional. A bed, a wardrobe and a sofa in the corner were the only furniture of note.

Amit shut the windows to drown out the external mayhem. Ignoring the growl of his tummy, as hunger pangs attacked him, he focused on the blades of the fan, which cut through the rays of streetlights slinking in from outside. Demon-like shadows danced on the ceiling to the tune of the squealing sirens.

Exhausted, Amit fell asleep. But his sleep was disrupted, and in the course of the night, he was jolted awake.

It was not a particularly hot night, but he found himself drenched in sweat. An eerie hush shrouded the room, cutting through the muffled car horns and stifled pandemonium of the street. The illuminated hands of the wall clock were at 10.40 p.m. He had been asleep for scarcely two hours.

Why am I feeling so drained?

A sinking feeling pervaded Amit's body. There was an uncomfortable undercurrent filling up the space around him, making him wary. He reached for his phone, and rubbing his eyes, he surveyed the room with its flashlight. The beam scanned the television trolley, the wardrobe, the corner table, and in due course, came to a standstill on the sofa not far from his bed.

What in God's name…?

Aghast, the phone fell from Amit's hand but still cast enough light for him to see clearly. His heart was thudding so loud that he could hear every single beat. There was someone sitting on the sofa. An old woman!

Who are you? Where did you come from? Am I dreaming?

Amit felt trapped in his own head. His body was frozen in fear. The woman sat there, looking fixedly at him. Her grey hair was like a halo, illuminating her chalky face. Her sari with faded paisleys was hitched up to her sagging calves. Her skin was like parchment paper, the protruding green veins bursting through the delicateness.

Who is she? Why is she here?

Amit tried to scream for help, but no sound came out. He mustered all his energy to raise himself up, but he was totally paralysed. Sweat was trickling down his face, sadistically tickling him as it ran its course.

It was only an old woman, but he had never seen anything so scary. How she got there was a mystery, but the way she looked as she sat there looking at him was even more petrifying. Her feet were dangling like broken branches from the edge of the sofa. The toes were misshapen and disfigured with age – the fungus-riddled, yellow toenails upturned.

Amit could not look away, even though his entire being was willing him to do so. It was like he was hypnotized and in thrall. Her matted white hair had attached itself protectively to her smashed head. Her concave skull looked like someone had carelessly scooped portions of her brain out. The cavernous indented wrinkles on her face were streaked with blood that had dripped down from the side of her cracked skull.

Please dear God, please let this be a dream. Let me wake up. Please.

Then, as her eyes blazed with sheer lunacy, the old woman rolled back her head and laughed. It sounded like a bolt of thunder ricocheting through the space. The place reverberated with what sounded like a sadistic mimicry of laughter. It was a booming sound that ripped his eardrums as it came at him from all the corners of the room.

Amit felt as if he was trapped in a loop of horror that went on and on. Her head swaying back and forth, back and forth.

Then, his eyes widened in terror as he felt a heavy weight on his chest.

It felt like someone was sitting on top of him, but the lady was still on the sofa, laughing. His belly cramped up as dread impaled him. He did not know how, but he knew she was controlling his body with her mind. The weight on his chest was testing his endurance.

Amit tried to climb off the bed. His recalcitrant body refused to budge. He tried to yell, but he had no voice.

He could only keep looking at her direction.

Stuck as he was, and unable to do anything about his predicament, Amit could not help but notice the finer details about his woman intruder. She was awfully old, older than any person he knew. To his twenty-six-year-old young mind, she seemed ancient. She was slightly-built, as if shrunken by age, but despite her skinny physique, she seemed to be dwarfing the room with her presence. Her head tilted from side-to-side quizzically, as her sunken eyes stared at him. They looked like the home of the damned.

Amit tried to shut his eyes, but couldn't.

The only thing his body seemed to be able to do was breathe, and he counted each shallow breath to soothe the terror engulfing him.

Go away! Go away!

The laughter. The stare. They went on and on.

Stop it!

Just when he thought he would go mad with the fear, silence came crashing down on the room. The weight eased off his chest. Precisely at that moment, the old woman vanished from the sofa. Amit glanced around the length and breadth of the room, terrified. The old woman was nowhere to be seen.

Amit gingerly moved his fingers, then his legs, and a rush of freedom overtook him as his body sprung back into action. His legs felt rubbery as he jumped out of bed and switched on the lights.

The clock showed 10.45 p.m.

Five minutes. That's it?

They would probably remain the longest and most terrifying five minutes Amit would experience in all his life. Till date, he can't get those eyes out of his head – those aloof, spiritless eyes. That insane laughter. That abyss.

After listening to Amit's story, I did some research on the dreadful tragedy on Lamington Road. I found that only one death had been reported – that of an 85-year-old landlady of the collapsed building, who had died due to fatal head injuries. His unwanted visitor had an identity. A fact that Amit Ramsay never knew, till I informed him recently. A fact and a fear that will now haunt him forever and after.

Night

That creature of the night.
That flickering light.
That strange click.
Who next will he pick?

The Hotel

Dharam Ramsay is the older son of the late Arjun Ramsay. He is not an active part of the film industry and has chosen to work in various other fields, including the hospitality industry.

Panchgani or 'The Land of Five Hills' is a hill station in Maharashtra, neighbouring the busy Mahabaleshwar. The British discovered it during pre-Independence days. The idyllic setting and all-year-round pleasant climate have helped Panchgani sustain its popularity, with an abundance of lodging and boarding options catering to the perennial flow of holidaymakers and weekend revellers.

In 2003, Dharam was working as a manager in a hotel in Panchgani. The property was near the highway and as it was reasonably priced, it attracted its fair share of visitors. The sleeping arrangements were adequate, the food satisfactory, and there was even a pool on the premises, which added to its appeal. The staff that worked there stayed in dormitory-style quarters, away from the main hotel. However, since he was the manager of the property, Dharam's room was adjacent to the reception, on the ground floor of the building. The owners lived in Mumbai and wanted a trustworthy manager, so Dharam shifted base from Mumbai to Panchgani to work full time.

It almost seems where there's a Ramsay, the supernatural must follow. From time to time, a random staff member or another would complain to Dharam about a supernatural entity sitting on his chest, exerting tremendous pressure and only letting go when the person had reached the point of suffocation. This invariably happened when the person was asleep. The employees were convinced about the existence of ghosts at the hotel. It scared quite a few of them away.

Despite the fast turnover of employees, a new person inevitably popped up narrating the same story – of being rendered immobile by a powerful, invisible force.

The true-blue Ramsay that he was, Dharam listened to the stories with rapt attention. He was not convinced by their claims of the hotel being haunted. He dismissed these accounts since they sounded almost identical, and he felt that it was mere gossip among the staff. Still, he diplomatically kept his scepticism aside while speaking to them. He reasoned that the outlying location of the hotel and the mystique of the night were playing tricks on people's minds. Mass hysteria could be quite prevalent in smaller towns.

Ghosts were part of Dharam's family business of films. But though he had grown up on a staple diet of horror stories, he had never personally experienced anything of the sort. So it was especially hard for him to believe the stories surrounding around the hotel.

Dharam's working hours were lengthy and hectic, and he looked forward to finally relaxing in his bedroom at night.

The layout of his room was basic but cosy. There were two single beds placed on the left and right sides of a centre table. Opposite the beds was a long table with drawers and a television set propped on it.

Dharam liked to sleep on the bed closer to the window; he enjoyed the fresh hillside air that swept into the room. He had got used to the frequent clamour of birds and insects that resided in the encompassing greenery. Living and working in Panchgani was a welcome change from the hectic life and pace in a congested, polluted city like Mumbai.

One night, like every other night, Dharam watched some television and was ready to retire. There was a nip in the air, and a gentle breeze blew in through the open window. The window was creaking mournfully on its hinges. A lizard, its nervous tongue flicking, bolted across the window frame. Having been on his feet all day, Dharam drifted off to sleep as soon as his head hit the pillow.

But that night, everything he had believed in – or hadn't – changed.

Dharam felt his blanket hitch, curling its way up slowly. He shuffled his feet in his sleep to tuck them back into the cushiness of the blanket. But the blanket rolled itself up again, exposing his ankles. He frowned in his sleep, as he felt a tightening around his ankles. He shifted a bit, still asleep; but the pressure around his ankles kept increasing.

Dharam woke up with a jolt when he finally felt as if someone had caught hold of his feet and was squashing them! 'Hey, stop! Who is it? Leave me!' he yelled, trying to throw off the person or thing that had his feet trapped in an icy, vice-like grip. It felt like a snake was winding its way up his legs, coiling itself around them tighter and tighter.

There was no person or creature in the room, but phantom hands were squeezing Dharam's ankles so hard, they hurt.

Along with the chill, monumental waves of fright enveloped his body.

The staff had warned him that the hotel was haunted, but Dharam had been too dismissive of the stories. Now, he would probably not even live to regret it.

Damn fool that I was!

But Dharam knew that even if he had listened and believed the tales, no heroics would work here.

Will they even find my body? How will anyone know what actually happened?

The lenient face of his father, Arjun Ramsay, came to his mind. Whatever the outcome, Dharam resolved that he was not going to give up without a fight.

He struggled and squirmed, trying to get out of the deadly grasp, but his body was being pulled viciously by his feet.

Where is it trying to take me? What fate worse than death is awaiting me? Will I be buried under mounds of soil alongside my devilish killer?

Dharam slumped momentarily to gain some strength, and then he yelled at the top of his voice. But his cry for help went unheard.

Trapped and terrified, Dharam noticed a moth flit in, but it was knocked out by his thrashing hands as he struggled to free himself.

The walls of his room were swaying with the shadows cast by the silvery oak tree outside his window. The temperature in the room kept dropping steadily. The room seemed to be getting colder by the second, till it seemed to him that it was ice cold. Dharam felt himself being dragged off the bed even as he tried to use every ounce of his strength to resist.

He fought to stay rooted to where he was.

He would not make this easy. His efforts were no longer focused on freeing himself; now, he just tried to stay still, on the bed, grappling for a hold to prevent whatever it was from pulling him off it. He was not going to die like a coward. He would fight till the end. He owed at least that much to his father.

Dharam was almost half off the bed when his legs were suddenly released, flung violently like the rubber band of a slingshot. And just like that, he was free.

What in God's name just happened? Why did it let go of me?

Without any delay, Dharam jumped from the bed and slammed the window shut. The unnerved lizard was catapulted outside, while its amputated tail plopped and wriggled on the floor.

Dharam put the lights on, eyeing the room. There was no sign of any trespasser. Nothing had been disturbed. But he could clearly see bruise marks on his ankles. He massaged them, shuddering at the thought of what had transpired. He double-checked to see if the windows were locked and then lay down on the bed – half-exhausted, half-relieved.

It seemed the phantom had left through the window from which it had entered. What if the entity came back again? How could he sleep now or tomorrow or the day after? He knew he needed to leave the bedroom so that he could get his bearings back.

As Dharam walked towards the lobby, the sleepy receptionist wondered what the manager was doing up and about at 4 a.m. But looking at Dharam's flushed yet wan face, the man understood without a word being exchanged.

The new manager had received his official welcome from the ghostly residents of the hotel.

Dharam remembers recounting his terrifying episode to the hotel owner. He also narrated the staff members' cases along with his own. The owner was an elderly man who was deeply religious. Since that time, every room of the hotel and the desk at the reception has kept a copy of a holy book. Did this help? Who knows? The last Dharam heard, the hauntings had stopped.

Alone

The living wipe each other's tears.
The dead weep but nobody hears.
Their souls struggle seeing us in pain
so they give up the chance to be born again.
We miss our loved ones who are gone;
but after a while, life must go on.
For them, there is no end in sight.
For us, they rejected the eternal light.

The Knock

Tanuja is the eldest daughter of the late Arjun Ramsay. She spent plenty of vacations holidaying at Ramsay film locations in her childhood years, till she got married at a very early age. Tanuja considers herself pretty dauntless. When she was young, a cousin dared her to enter a graveyard alone in the night, and she did.

The year 2012 was a testing period for Tanuja. She lost her mother, Rajkumari, to a prolonged illness. Life slowly limped back to normal, but Tanuja acutely felt the loss of her mother.

Nearly a year later, it began.

Tanuja habitually slept late, usually post 3 a.m. She was used to watching television and then dozing off. Her stress levels were very high at the time, so sleep was evasive. Bored with switching channels on the television, Tanuja dimmed the lights in an attempt to try and get some shut eye. Failing at that, she tried meditating, by focusing on a speck on the wall, craving to soothe her hyperactive mind.

She noticed a spider scaling the cobweb it had built on the ceiling. Its hairy legs were hanging on to the silky threads rather precariously, looking ready to fall at any moment.

Thak-thak!

Tanuja jumped in fright.

It was past 3.30 a.m. Who could be knocking at this time, that too on her bedroom door?

She staggered out of bed, puzzled at the disturbance at this late an hour. She opened the bedroom door with trepidation.

The night light was glowing weakly, encircled by a gloomy halo. The passageway was empty. There was nobody out there.

Baffled, Tanuja ran back to her bed. The draft from the air-conditioner draft was wintry now. Her blanket was unable to keep the cold from seeping into her very bones.

She switched off the air-conditioner, but that didn't help. The room was getting progressively colder.

Am I coming down with the flu?

Her teeth began to chatter, and she slid under the blanket.

Thak-thak!

That same knock again. The nerve-racking sound was scaring the living daylights out of her.

Thak-thak!

Persistent and insistent, the knock echoed in her ears.

Tanuja's eyes darted from left to right frantically. She listened intently to the assertive sound, trying to gauge its source.

The sound seemed to be coming from inside her cupboard now.

What? How? Is this someone's idea of a joke? Is there somebody hiding inside the cupboard? A thief?

Tanuja's stomach was tied up in knots at the mental image of a violent, murderous robber.

Nausea caused bitter bile to rise to her throat, and she strived to swallow it back. *Why would a thief knock and alert me?*

Grabbing the alarm clock at her bedside, in case she needed to use it as a weapon, Tanuja yanked the cupboard open. Half expecting a gun-wielding assassin, she was flummoxed to find absolutely nothing inside. She had not even registered how much her hands had been shaking. She looked through the room and hovered around the cupboard aimlessly, wondering if she could figure out where the sound had come from.

The knocking had stopped, so she returned to her bed. As she struggled to fall sleep, Tanuja promised herself to stop watching horror films when she was alone. She noticed that the spider had moved lower down the wall. If he came close, she would whack it, she thought to herself.

Thak-thak! Thak, thak, thak.

Tanuja was starting to lose her nerve. There it was again!

This time, the sound came from the cupboard on the other side of the room.

The windows were fastened. The door was latched. *Were there rats? Could rats even knock?* Thoughts flitted through Tanuja's mind in rapid succession, but she barely registered them. What was going on? Was she hallucinating? Was there something wrong with her ears? She covered her head with her pillow in exasperation, wanting to tear her hair out.

Thak-thak-thak.

It was a muted tap, but it was unmistakable. Eventually, it tapered off.

What if the room is haunted? Utter nonsense! It must be a plumbing issue.

Tanuja decided to get it checked the next day.

The knocking continued intermittently through the week. There was no likely source that she could find, but the tapping sounds were unmistakable. But there was no way she was going to entertain the thought of ghosts again.

After she got over her initial fright, Tanuja started to ignore the knocking. After all, there was no earthly explanation for it. But what was notable was that it never happened in the presence of others, and she could find no solution to the problem.

The knocking usually came in the dead of the night from inside one of the cupboards – as if someone was trapped behind the panel.

Now sort of accustomed to the knocking, Tanuja tried to find a pattern to it, though it seemed totally random in its timing. There was always an unendurable frigidity in the room as soon as the knocking began. But when the sound stopped, the temperature went back to normal.

Most people's minds shut out things they cannot understand. Tanuja, too, accepted the situation as one of those mysteries, and she kept it to herself. The probability of the room being haunted by spirits did cross her mind frequently, but it seemed too silly an idea, especially since horror was the family business.

For her own peace of mind, Tanuja blocked out any notion of troubled spirits haunting her. Besides, there did not seem to be any malice behind the knocking and she reasoned that there was not much she could do about it anyway.

The nights progressed fitfully to the rhythm of the knocking. It had now become a regular feature in her life and seemed almost normal somehow.

Things started to go downhill for Tanuja in 2016. She went through a rough patch in her personal life. Then, in January 2019, tragedy reared its ugly head again. This time, Tanuja lost her father, Arjun.

In his last days, Arjun Ramsay expressed unceasing worry about his daughter's plight. She was invariably on his mind. The stress may well have sent his heart into self-destruct mode.

Tanuja was reeling with Arjun's loss in the midst of her personal crisis. How would she make it through life with neither parent? Who would she turn to when the going got tougher?

One night, soon after her father's death, she was in bed when she heard a single knock.

Thak!

This knock sounded completely different from the earlier ones, and it was coming from right under her bed.

The knock shook her. The inevitable cold set in, along with abject terror.

How much more could her wracked nerves take? Tanuja wanted to scream, but she pulled the blanket over her head and plugged her ears with her fingers. *Shut up. Shut up. Shut up.*

Thak.

There it was again. A single loud knock.

Thak.

The emotional upheaval of the past few days had drained her physically and mentally, but Tanuja was determined not to crumble under the strain.

Gathering all her courage, she threw off the blanket and cautiously peeked under the bed. Nothing. The hollow space underneath the bed and the firm foundation on which the mattress lay was all that she could see.

The nipping cold penetrating through the numbness was all that she could feel.

With all the bizarre goings-on, Tanuja accepted the possibility of the impossible. As if on cue, yet another peculiar event occurred.

Tanuja had a much-adored German Shepherd puppy, Leo. She beckoned the animal to her. But Leo stepped back, away from her, scared and cowering. The more she tried to coax him to come towards her, the further he backed away. The whimpering animal refused to take his eyes off Tanuja or budge in her direction.

Tanuja was bewildered by his reaction. This had never happened before. Animals are known to have a sense of the unknown.

She believes Leo had seen something that terrified the otherwise fierce yet playful puppy, who was always rushing towards her. What was it around her that had scared Leo so much?

To this day, Tanuja remains plagued by the incomprehensible. Periodically it happens, a knock, only one, for some time from under the bed on which she sleeps. The knock, though faint, can be heard only by her, sometimes in the day, but mostly at night.

Tanuja now finds the sound to be strangely soothing in its regularity. She has tried talking to whatever it is that is making the sound, but it is impossible to communicate, since the entity speaks a different tongue.

When she lies awake alone, Tanuja cannot help but wonder if someone is trying to make contact with her – someone who has no other means of communication.

Dead people don't talk, but perhaps they knock.

Arjun Ramsay's death was rather sudden. Between 2012 and 2019, Tanuja and her husband had lost both sets of parents. The earlier knocking had started after her mother's passing. This new one after her father's demise. Was the knocking one of them – or neither? The single, subdued and gentle knock was so reminiscent of Arjun Ramsay's personality. Maybe Arjun has been trying to reassure his only daughter that he will watch over her unfailingly, even after his death. But how does one ever know?

Entombed

The houses, they speak.
Loud whispers, they leak.
Walls that plead.
Insides that bleed.
Most people cannot see
the spirits' angry plea.

The Palace

An essential ingredient of creating the ambience in a horror movie is the physical setting. But what happens when the location is so haunted that it feels like you are a character in a horror film yourself instead? One palace, so many frightened Ramsays!

Set on multi-acres of land, the 'Palace' is an intriguing blend of Mughal and Gothic architecture. It is perched on the edge of a cliff and offers scintillating views of the Arabian Sea as well as the surrounding village. The tombs of the owners' ancestors are also part of the landscape. In short, it is the ideal setting for horror and became part of quite a few of the Ramsay brand of scary movies.

On the invitation of her brothers, Asha grabbed the opportunity to spend some time with the Ramsay family on location. Her younger daughter, Jaya, who was around ten-years-old then, tagged along with her. Since a major portion of the shooting would take place in the wee hours of the night, the day offered ample opportunity to explore the area.

It was an idle morning, and ambling around with Jaya, Asha came across a dilapidated well. A thick layer of moss had staked its claim on the structure, and ants were navigating their way through its velvety topography.

'What is that, Mamma?' A city-bred child, Jaya had never seen a well before.

'It's a well. It is very deep and stores water. Come, let me show you – but be careful.'

Holding her daughter's hand, Asha guided her towards the well. Both mother and daughter peered within its yawning depth. But nothing could have prepared them for the nightmare before their eyes.

Standing in the dry well was a giant of a creature. The large being was inches away and his bloodshot eyes were glowering at the mother–daughter duo. Just below his matted hair, a bulging vein throbbed angrily. The creature lunged at them, arms outstretched.

Asha screamed and grabbed her terrified daughter.

Stumbling over the uneven pebbles, the pair ran from there. They did not dare to look behind. Jaya could not keep up with her mother's speed and fell down crying. Asha lifted her up swiftly and wiped her grazed knee. Asha's stomach hurt from the frantic running and the weight of carrying her wailing daughter in her arms, but she kept going.

Only when the well was far behind them did she pause for breath. It took her forever to convince her terror-stricken daughter that it was probably her uncles playing a prank on them. What else could Asha offer as an explanation? It was the only one that made sense to her at that moment to pacify the crying child, even as she grappled with the petrifying reality of what she had just seen.

As Asha and Jaya approached the palace, they saw that the preparation for the shooting was on in full swing. In an attempt to take the fear out of her daughter's system, Asha took her to the makeup area, where the Ramsay monster was being readied for the shot. Jaya became hysterical, and Asha stood rooted to the ground in astonishment.

In front of them, getting his makeup done, was a monster identical to the one in the well! The only difference was that this one was smiling at them. The actor's cosmetic fangs were dangling over his cracked lips as he held out his oversized hand to Jaya, who hid behind her mother.

'Don't be afraid, little girl. This is only makeup. See?' He offered the costume-less part of his arm to alleviate her fears.

Jaya shunned the actor's kind gesture. The incongruity between the actor's mollifying words and his booming voice was unsettling. She clenched Asha's sweaty palm even tighter.

'Were you in the well a little while ago? Practising for a scene?' Asha asked, hoping against hope that the actor would answer in the affirmative.

'Well? What well? I have been here getting ready for more than an hour now. Why? Did something happen?'

'No, no! It's nothing. You carry on, or the shooting will be delayed. Jaya, say bye to the nice uncle. See, it's only makeup. There are no monsters.'

But the unrelenting child spurned any conciliatory move made by her concerned mother or the congenial monster.

For Jaya, this became a defining moment. To this day, she blocks out any talk of ghosts, monsters and the supernatural. She senses their presence but denies their existence. She is still hiding from her own bogeyman.

Asha and Jaya were not the only Ramsays to have blood-curdling experiences at the palace. Gopal Ramsay, the son of the senior-most Ramsay brother, Kumar, had his own sinister account.

The caretaker had warned the family to avoid the terrace after dark since there were rumours of a supernatural presence. Another area out of bounds was one of the rooms in the Palace. It was padlocked, but a shuffling sound of feet could often be heard from within. The caretaker claimed it was his sister, who was mentally unstable, so they never let anyone into the room.

But Gopal, being inquisitive, snuck into the passage one night and peeked through the keyhole. He could hear the shuffling but couldn't see anybody in the room. At that very moment, the thick glass of the window in the passageway cracked and then shattered.

Scared witless, Gopal raced away and never ventured near that room or the passageway ever again.

Tanuja Ramsay, too, remembers many a night when she and other members of the family heard demonic screams of a woman coming from the Palace. On enquiring about it, she was told that a woman had gone insane after her lover had left her, so she was locked away in one of the rooms. Different explanations – but the same unadulterated fear.

The spooky residents of the Palace do not just haunt the Ramsays. They spare no one – not even unwitting outsiders. Once, a character artiste in a movie, who was living at the Palace, found himself being throttled in his sleep. Caught between dream and reality, he could not figure out which was which, as he grappled to save himself. To his shock, he woke up the next morning on the floor of the room, without a clue as to how he had gotten there.

The palace no longer opens its doors to the public. The formidable iron gates keep people away. It stands majestic and alone, pensively surveying the servile sea.

But the questions remain unanswered to this day.

Who was that mysterious woman?

Did the actor playing the monster know his barbaric character from the film had a twin from another world residing in the Palace?

Did the makeup artist or the director base the monster on their own gruesome encounter with the real one whom Asha and Jaya had met?

No one knows. The only thing that is known is that this monster, who was named Saamri, went on to become the Ramsay Brothers' most iconic archfiend.

Sunrise

The dead outnumbered the living.
The night uniting both worlds.
The living in their beds,
the dead in their graves.
Their reluctance, the only difference.
Like diffident children forced into sleeping earlier,
The mischievous ghosts creep out in the dark.
Then the sunrise prayers put them back to sleep.
The collective meditation of human voices,
drowning the screams of their suffering souls.
Till the next night.
And the next.

Three Generations of Terror

Intuitive. Empath. Receiver. These are words that have been used to describe me by an assortment of people with psychic abilities, even before they got to know my predispositions. Despite my mother's umpteen ghostly encounters, I failed to connect the dots. But when my younger daughter, Tiana, began experiencing supernatural occurrences, I saw the prominent line connecting the three generations. It was not a coincidence that my mother, my daughter and I had heightened intuition and experiences with spirits. The extrasensory gene has been known to pass down from generation to generation. There was no external influence on us to direct us towards the discovery of this second sight. In fact, it was a taboo topic to discuss with young, impressionable minds. Yet, each one of us individually had several brushes with the paranormal.

Does it run in families, this unique gift?

Based on my experience, the answer is a resounding yes. Does everyone in the family share this capability? No.

In my side of the Ramsay family tree, the ability seemed to have passed down from my mother to me and then to my younger daughter, Tiana; and to an extent, my sister, Jaya, and her pre-teen daughter, Thea. Surprisingly, however, a fair number of Ramsays had come into contact with the spirit world in some way or another.

Gopal Ramsay, Kumar Ramsay's eldest son, once saw a cyclist in his path while he was being driven on a deserted Mahabaleshwar road. He told the driver to be careful but the cyclist vanished before their eyes. A confounded Gopal turned around to see him cycling away, having mysteriously bypassed their car.

Jaya, who after much persuasion, reluctantly opened up about her occult experiences of a woman's ghost that has haunted her since childhood. Earlier, the spirit used to chase her down the corridor of her house till she scuttled to the refuge of her bedroom. Now, the same woman appears in the bathroom mirror of her married home. Jaya avoids looking in the mirror as much as she can, because she knows the woman is waiting for her. She has patiently been hanging on for Jaya since the very beginning.

Jaya's daughter Thea, speaking independently, refers to the same bathroom mirror. Once, she saw a reflection of a wolf-like creature and its indented claw marks on the mirror. She bolted from the bathroom but the next morning, the mirror was flawless again. Thea also recalls an incident when she was around six years old. She noticed the shadow of a woman walking alongside hers. She could feel faint breathing on her neck, but there was nobody else around. This happened on quite a few occasions and the shadow went away after a while but left its murky memory behind.

The late Arjun Ramsay made light of an eerie encounter in print. His daughter, Tanuja, and sister, Asha, believe that there was more to that incident than he expressed. It was around 3 a.m., and he was waiting for the crew to pack up after a long night of shooting at a graveyard. He went running when he heard the screams of the crew members. A man had fallen into a casket while carrying a very heavy spotlight. He was yelling for help because he thought the corpse within had caught hold of his foot. Arjun laughingly rescued the man, but when he tried to get out himself, he felt the body inside seize his own foot. He managed to shake it off and get out of the casket. Later, Arjun chalked down the episode to a clumsy entanglement with the rattling bones of a skeleton. Originally, however, he had confided in Asha about the potential reality of that distinctly scary experience. Later, presumably in denial, it became just a humorous anecdote for him.

How many other Ramsays and their descendants have gone through these paranormal escapades? There must undoubtedly be more than the ones we know of, but some have been muted by the irrevocability of death and yet others by the daunting prospect of admission. Who decided to grant us this rare field of vision? Was it random selection by the universe, a quirk of destiny, or part of a grand plan? As a family we have far too many engagements with spirits to sweep these events under the rug.

Why did the Ramsay Brothers choose horror as their speciality? Or was it horror that chose them? Was there even a choice? Is there a calling they have had over and above making scary films, which needed to be fulfilled? Why does the supernatural come naturally to us? Did the House of Ramsays rest on the fault-line of fate that unearthed buried confidences of the spirit world?

Instinctively, I feel the unknown selected us and there has to be a reason for it. We must embrace this awareness rather than live in fear of it. The quest for knowledge of the afterlife spans infinity. Who knows what lies beyond? The only certainty is that spirits are drawn to us more than to most others, and evading that gospel truth might just drive us away from the potential for enlightenment.

The only certainty is that spirits are drawn to us and evading that gospel truth will drive us away from the potential for enlightenment.

Encroaching

We would have no grouse
if you just left our house.
But if you choose to stay
then we will make you pay.
Our presence you will feel
for it is our solitude you steal.

The Bungalow

Devidas Thawani, better known as Deva, is married to Maya (Asha) Ramsay. Deva and his father, the late Jotumal Thawani, were in the business of financing films. They were associated with the financing of dozens of blockbuster films and had ties with a lot of successful Bollywood producers. Originally in the stationery business, they were motivated to dive further into the world of films by Asha's father, F.U. Ramsay.

Houses, like people, have energy. They can be as welcoming as a mother's embrace or as stifling as a hangman's noose. A home carries the weight of both, the joy and the sadness of its residents. The walls are solemn keepers of secrets. Some houses are doomed while others are blessed.

Our destinies often become intertwined with the places where we live.

Housewarming ceremonies or elaborate prayers are usually conducted when one buys a new home, in an attempt to drive away misfortune or appease the remnants of negative forces. Yet, despite our best efforts, some homes are besieged with evil and drag us down to the depths of the netherworld.

The 'bungalow' was one such place of unmitigated malevolence. It was at a spectacular location, a prime piece of property right on Juhu Beach. The sand kissed the base of its raised walls and the sea frolicked a few steps away. It was next to impossible to get this kind of property in Mumbai. And even if one did, the cost would be astronomical.

Nothing in life comes without a price and all its owners learned this the hard way.

According to some stories, a prosperous diamond trader had bought this dream home and, following that, sustained huge losses in his business. In absolute desperation, he had then sold it to a film producer. The delighted producer had moved into his palatial residence after spending a great deal of money on its renovation.

Built in contemporary Indo-Western style, the house had three levels. Another film producer had leased the upper level and terrace. In the basement was a gymnasium, steam, sauna, jacuzzi, and a television room with a billiards table. The first level had a mammoth living room, dining room, prayer room and kitchen. The second level had three bedrooms. Outside, there was a garden with a hammock, an outdoor whirlpool and a bar.

Soon after moving into this paradise, life turned dismal for the producer as he underwent incomprehensible financial failures just like the previous owner did. When this producer found himself in debt, Deva lent him money. The producer assured Deva that he would pay him back, but in the interim, offered him the bungalow to use. He needed a few days to pack up and move out, and he did not want to sell or lease the house to the other producer who lived there because of previous conflicts between them. Deva and his family seized the opportunity to get such a luxurious second home.

The year 2006 was the beginning of a very memorable time for Deva and his family, filled with happy times living in the bungalow. It became regular practice to travel from the house in South Mumbai to Juhu for the weekend. Asha, especially, spent many weeks there.

But gradually, the demonic presence in the house slithered into the lives of the family.

As much as the family enjoyed being there, for some of us, there was a disagreeable aura in the bungalow. My mother developed health problems; my father faced personal and financial losses. After three years since we were given access, the producer sold the bungalow in 2009 and repaid my father. As much as we hated and resisted the prospect of losing the bungalow, it was probably the smartest move my father made. Not financially, of course, because the bungalow was worth a lot more than its selling price. However, it was a white elephant and its utility value did not justify the amount of money blocked in its ownership and upkeep. Along with being a big budget property, its unlucky reputation preceded it. Since property buyers are by and large a superstitious lot, the offers were sporadic.

But the deed was done. My father had been paid in full, and we vacated the property and moved. We did so with a heavy heart. The new owner, a mutual fund manager, moved in. Almost straightaway, his charmed life came undone. He was forced to resign from his prestigious position and was slammed with legal cases. Under duress, he had to sell to the nearest available buyer – the film producer residing in the upper levels, bought over the place he had so coveted. He now owned the entire property.

The producer continues to live there, but he has developed critical health issues and his family life has been torn apart with internal conflicts. The bungalow has spared none of its inhabitants to date. There are whispers of bad Vaastu, of the effect of suicides in the neighbouring building, including that of the famous actress Parveen Babi.

Having lived there myself, I believe that the ground itself is tainted with death. A senior employee at the location told us that this portion of the beach was used as a cremation ground back when burning bodies in the open was allowed. He had also heard that this was an actual graveyard site that had been destroyed to make way for property construction.

Perhaps, that is why the bungalow strikes back – sparing none of its residents, ruining their lives, filling them with woe.

There are no weapons against the anger of the dead. Their resting place had been defiled, and the spirits wreaked havoc to reclaim what was theirs. The ashes of the departed are mingled in the very foundation of the bungalow. Upon their desecration, people have built their dreams. Why then would they not strike back at us – the intruders, the ones who violated their home?

Despite the failed financial deal, a friendship was forged between my father and the film producer. Later, after the bungalow had left all our lives, I asked him and his wife if they had ever felt the evil that shrouded the bungalow. The producer told me that after he had given possession to my father, in less than a month, he gained a huge financial windfall. Subsequently, his life got back on track.

His wife's words still echo in my ears: 'Everyone who came to that house would be enchanted by its beauty and tell us how lucky we were to call it ours. All I felt for the time that I lived there was a relentless feeling of unease. It never did feel like home. Only when I left the house, to go shopping or meet a friend, did I feel free, like a massive weight had been lifted from over me.'

Asha and the Bungalow

The lure of the sea had always been irresistible to Asha. Living in her primary residence at Marine Drive was a godsend because she loved strolling by the seaside. When the Juhu bungalow fell into her lap, she snatched the opportunity to spend time there and enjoy the proximity to the water. Her husband, Deva, joined her often, but most of her time at the bungalow was spent with her sister, Kamla.

Asha knew that there was something inauspicious about the bungalow, something she could not pinpoint. However, as was her approach towards life, she took matters lightly and chose to enjoy the place.

It was common practice for her to invite her brothers and their wives to spend time there. Tulsi Ramsay, not much older than Asha, was very close to her. He and his wife, Kanta, stayed there often.

One area of the house that gave Asha the creeps was the basement. She would never venture there unaccompanied, even though it housed the gymnasium and she loved working out. The television room, with its projector and mega-sized screen, was in the basement, too. She would watch films there, but always in the company of family and friends.

On one of Tulsi's visits, Asha, Tulsi and Kanta went to the basement to watch a film. The wall was an audio-visual canvas splashed with images from the projected screen. The movie buffs sank into the plush chairs.

Asha was in the front, and the couple was sitting behind her. Asha was thoroughly engrossed in the movie, when a soft gust of air caressed the base of her neck. She disregarded it, thinking it was a draft from the air-conditioner.

Then, a shadow swirled within the colours on the screen. The whiff of air was now moving languidly across the breadth of Asha's back. Goosebumps perforated her skin, as an unseen presence zoomed past her armchair. Nervously, she turned around, only to find Tulsi and Kanta missing.

Where have they gone?

Asha clutched the handles of her chair tightly and wondered if she should make a run for it. The light from the projector streamed through the shadow like a knife through butter. The bulbs in the room were flickering erratically. Asha crawled off the chair and ran up the stairs as fast as she could.

Her brother and his wife were in the living room picking up some snacks.

'Why did you go off without telling me?' she chided them for leaving her alone.

'You were so engrossed in the movie. We thought we would get the snacks and come down. Relax. Why the fuss?'

No fuss. Just a ghost!

But Asha decided not to say anything.

The incident confirmed to her that she had been right all along ... that there was something in the house. A presence. Without company, the basement was to be bypassed at all cost.

Like her daughter, Jaya, who had a similar spooky experience, she would soon get to know that the basement was not the only place, with unwanted company.

One night, Asha was fast asleep in the master bedroom of the bungalow. Her sister, Kamla, was feeling unwell and did not want to sleep in the air-conditioned room. She had decided to use the other bedroom. The master bedroom was the best room in the house, with French windows that offered an uninhibited view of the sea. It was late and the uplifting, rhythmic lapping of the waves was the only sound that could be heard. It was routine for Asha to wake up in the night to use the bathroom. Her slippers always lay on the side of her bed since she did not like walking barefoot.

That night too, Asha woke up to use the bathroom. But when she groggily looked for her slippers, she could only find one of the pair.

Where can it be? What a nuisance!

Asha bent down and looked under the bed, but it was not there. There was no way she was walking barefoot to the bathroom. The glacial marble floor stung the soles of her feet as she trudged around the bed looking for the missing slipper. After a while, she found it placed neatly on the other side of the bed.

How did it get there?

Too drowsy to inconvenience herself with figuring out how the slipper had ended up there, she went to the bathroom and returned to bed.

Just as she was about to fall back into sleep, she was jolted into wakefulness.

Click. Hisssssss. Crackle.

The television had come on by itself. The ear-splitting static and blinding snow-like dots on the television jarred her nerves.

What on earth...?

Asha thought she was going berserk. She tried to calm herself. *Maybe I switched it on accidentally. Where's the remote?* Panicked, Asha searched for it. It lay idly on the bedside table. She switched off the television, and it died down with a vicious hiss. Her pulse was galloping furiously in unbridled dread. She had no doubt that this was the handiwork of a supernatural being.

But fear was not an option, so she decided to plunge headlong and speak to the entity.

Gathering her wits, she addressed the spirit in her typical, undaunted fashion. 'Hello there. Are you playing games with me? Do you want to talk to me? Do you want to be my friend? You can speak to me.'

She waited with bated breath, but there was no response.

'I have not hurt you in any way, so please do not trouble me. I am trying to sleep. You should sleep, too. I am requesting you, please. I am very tired. Good night!'

Asha spoke calmly, with a composure she was definitely not feeling. Bracing herself, she waited for a reaction, but none came. It was quiet after that. How silly she felt talking to spirits and expecting a reply!

Having had her fill of scares, Asha decided to go to Kamla's bedroom to spend the rest of the night. She was determined to never sleep by herself in the bedroom again, if she could help it. Even if the spirits could not frighten her away from the bungalow, she had grasped enough to know that one must never challenge the dead. Her stance was to treat them with respect, perhaps even more than the living.

When Asha and Kamla lived in the bungalow, they had a caretaker called Ramesh. He managed the place and lived there at night. Ramesh would lock up the house and sleep in the staff quarters outside the bungalow. The sisters would usually watch television, lock the bedroom door and retire to bed around midnight.

Kamla was ignorant about the creepy goings-on in the bungalow. Asha kept it so, since she was well-acquainted with her sister's faint-hearted personality.

One particular day, past midnight, the doorbell rang.

The sisters were startled. Who could it possibly be at this hour?

But the tring of the doorbell was unmistakable, and it rang persistently.

Was it Ramesh?

But Ramesh had the house key, so there was no reason for him to ring the bell. Perhaps the family upstairs had an emergency.

The sisters weren't sure what to do. Neither of them wanted to leave the confines of the bedroom to find out who was ringing the bell at such an unearthly hour. After a while, the ringing stopped. They heaved a sigh of relief.

The very next second, however, dread accosted them.

Thump. Thump. Thump.

They heard footfalls.

Was someone coming up the stairs? Who was making that racket?

The sound of the footsteps was palpably audible in the quiet of the night. It seemed like a gigantic creature was walking up the stairs. Kamla, dizzy with fear, clung to Asha. Asha wanted to open the door a wee bit to see who was outside, but Kamla held her back. The reverberation of the footsteps approached their bedroom door and stopped. Petrified, Asha and Kamla half-expected the door to be smashed open. The seconds crawled, and then everything was still.

Asha dialled Ramesh on the off-chance it had been him. But his groggy voice gave away that he had been fast asleep for a long time.

Who could that have been?

A million thoughts, spoken and unspoken, hurtled through their minds as they sat frozen. At long last, with the lights switched on, they went to bed hugging each other, like they did as little girls years ago.

Asha and her husband were very friendly with their neighbours at Marine Drive – Yasmin. Once, Yasmin accepted their invitation to spend the weekend at the bungalow.

Asha and she slept in the master bedroom. Cosy in the bed, the women had a delightful time chatting about the lovely day they had spent together. Then, they dozed off.

The next morning, Deva, Asha's husband, was up early. He was eating breakfast when he heard the bedroom door slam. Seconds later, Yasmin came running down the stairs, babbling incoherently. Her face was ashen and dripping with sweat, as she kept gesticulating towards the master bedroom.

'Devaji! Devaji!'

'What happened, Yasmin? Are you okay?'

'Devaji! Ashaji!'

Hearing the commotion, Asha woke up and came down from the bedroom. She touched her friend's arm but to her surprise, Yasmin recoiled from her touch.

Deva offered Yasmin some water, and slowly, she managed to pull herself together to narrate her ordeal.

'I woke up and glanced at Ashaji to see if she was awake.' Yasmin's mouth was twitching agitatedly in strenuous recollection. 'Ashaji was staring back at me, only the face was not of Ashaji but that of a demon. Devaji, I am telling you Ashaji had turned into a monster. I ran away from her!'

Asha kept quiet. What could she tell her sceptical husband about this house, about its spectral tenants? Deva would mock her just like he was making fun of Yasmin at that moment.

'How much wine did you have last night, Yasmin?' Deva cackled. 'This is what happens when you sleep next to the horror sister!'

'Devaji, it is not a joke! I am telling you, it was not Ashaji but a demon! I am going home right now. I am sorry. I cannot stay here another minute!'

That was the last time Yasmin ever entered the bungalow.

For three years, Asha stayed at the bungalow for months on end. The hallmark of her personality has always been acceptance. What cannot be cured must be endured is her dictum. In her handling of all situations in life, she stands firm, deals with things and moves on to the next chapter – be it man or ghost.

Alisha and the Bungalow

As much as I loved going to the bungalow, I felt a foreboding whenever I was in it. Like my mother, I could not figure out why I felt this way. I did not think too much of it nor cared to talk about it. At the time, I had not yet sufficiently explored the mysteries of the other world.

As time passed and the novelty wore off, my visits to the bungalow decreased. The primary reason I kept going back was to spend time with my parents – chiefly, my mother, who lived there more than she lived in her actual home at Marine Drive.

My daughters, Sascha and Tiana, enjoyed the mini vacations there, so that was an added bonus. Despite the holiday mood of sun and sand, I do not think I slept well for even a single night at the bungalow. My sleep would be disrupted; I would have floating dreams.

One morning, I woke up as the sun rose. This never happened in my own home, since I am not an early riser. The hands of the clock showed 6.35 a.m., and they were stuck at that time without the seconds hand moving. I kept staring at the clock face, wondering if the mechanism was faulty or the battery was dead. I went back to sleep and the clock was back to normal when I finally woke up.

What was uncanny was that this was happening almost every morning during that period of my stay at the bungalow. Every morning, the same: I was roused awake. It was always 6.35 a.m. The hands of the clock stayed motionless indefinitely and then were back to normal later.

Time literally stood still in that brief span while I was up. I got so used to this strange phenomenon that, after a while, I stopped wondering about it.

Soon after, my suspicions about the negative energy of the house were confirmed, and with hair-raising precision. One morning, I was roused from my slumber by a drilling sound, very much like a helicopter propeller. The din kept getting louder and louder, like a machine boring into my eardrums.

My husband, being the heavy sleeper that he is, was undisturbed. I nudged him, but he simply rolled over. I rubbed my groggy eyes and turned towards the window from where the sound seemed to be coming. There was a small balcony outside and what I saw made my jaw drop!

There was a luminous glow spreading in the room. At the centre was a blinding white light, a large globule. It was irregularly shaped, resembling a colossal amoeba.

Is it a UFO?

I sat up as miniature flashes of lightning struck my eyes; the brightness of the unidentifiable orb was dazzling. But despite the radiance, I could make out the unevenness of the edges. It was like a profusion of contours merged together in an immense, shapeless mass.

My first instinct was to reach out to figure out if it was real. Before I could react, however, it had dispersed. I never saw it again after that.

Today, when I think back, I wonder if that white light was a mass of spirits fused in mystic unison.

The feeling I had when in the bungalow remained consistent throughout. It was the ominous sense of being watched. The irrational need to look over my shoulder. I would avoid climbing up or down the staircase at night. Most of all, I could never bring myself to go unescorted to the basement. The area meant for recreation and relaxation gave me inexplicable jitters. Out of fear of ridicule, none of us expressed this reluctance churning within. We went along with the illusion of normalcy. Perhaps if we had expressed our misgivings, we would have had to throw away the key to the bungalow and, with it, our precious moments there. That could have been one reason for our reticence, making us stay loyal to rationality.

Fate had wed us into a marriage with this place. It felt like a corpse in a resplendent bridal gown. But when you lifted the opulent veil, you would see the heart of darkness and the face of hell.

Tiana and the Bungalow

The weekends were very exciting for my daughters, Sascha and Tiana, ever since the family began going to the bungalow. It was a welcome break from school days and the perfect place to finish homework. Asha looked forward to Friday evenings when her granddaughters filled the house with the joy that only children can bring.

Tiana, the younger one, who was ten years old at the time, loved exploring the place – running through all the rooms, going up and down the staircase. Her favourite part of the house was the upstairs bedroom with an elephantine mattress, designed to fit in at least six people. She would jump on it, turn cartwheels and roll across its length.

One Sunday, Tiana was reading a book in the room. She felt thirsty, so she decided to go down to the kitchen for a drink. As she came out of the room, she stopped in her tracks. Positioned on the top of the staircase was a woman – a stranger.

Tiana smiled tentatively at her, but the woman's face remained stony. She was really aged and looked like a holographic manifestation in white. She stood there, standing guard at the railing, like a lifeless marble statue.

Tiana's terror-stricken, childish mind cautioned her that this was no ordinary person, that she should get far away from the ghostly figure, just like she did from flying cockroaches. Clenching her tiny fists, she ran past the lady, almost falling down the staircase as she darted to the living room below.

Asha was in the living room and saw her granddaughter running frantically down the stairs. Tiana's lips had lost all colour and her face was waxen. She was biting her fingernails nervously.

'Naani, Naani. There is a scary lady on the staircase.'

Holding the trembling child in her arms, Asha tried to convince her that there was nobody there besides them.

'Tiana, did you have a bad dream? Come with me, and I will show you there is no lady there.'

Asha led the unwilling child up the flight of stairs to appease her. Tiana was still trembling. Asha wondered what had scared her so much. When they reached the spot, it was empty.

'See? No lady,' Asha said. 'Always remember to pray to God when you are scared.'

Tiana did not seem convinced and looked around suspiciously. She kept clinging to her grandmother. Not long after, Asha would find out that it was not a child's vivid imagination but horrifying reality.

After this incident, a perpetually tense Tiana would scurry up the stairs till she crossed the corridor leading to the bedroom. She would see the spectre every now and then, standing in the exact spot, at the foot of the spiral staircase. Tiana would always feel the same abject fear, but she would pray as her grandmother had taught her.

Luckily, children have a short memory. In time, Tiana forgot all about the lady and went back to having fun with her sister. The basement was the entertainment centre of the house. The girls would wear their swimming costumes to use the jacuzzi and the steam room.

The memories of the lady in white had stayed forgotten, until she began to show up again.

Sascha was changing into her clothes and Tiana was relaxing in the jacuzzi. There, she saw the lady again. The yellow spotlights were perforating her glassy outline. The woman stood there, watching her keenly. Tiana gawked at her, riveted with fear, hugging her tiny knees to her chest.

As soon as Sascha came out of the changing room, the woman disappeared.

On another occasion, the girls were watching a movie together. Sascha went to get some snacks for them. Tiana sat curled up in the armchair, waiting for her to return. The film was paused. Suddenly, the old woman appeared in front of the screen, its glare blending with her white silhouette as she walked past.

White on petrifying white!

As soon as Sascha returned to the room, the lady melted away, leaving Tiana gaping.

For all the fun activities the basement held, Tiana now hated going there for obvious reasons. Yet, she couldn't stop going down there without telling her sister about the scary lady. But Tiana was afraid to do that, thinking she would be teased for being a baby.

Though the sisters shared almost everything, the spine-chilling encounters with the white lady were Tiana's skeleton in the cupboard and remained locked away for a long time.

The spirits had made their first, but definitely not their last, appearance to the third generation of the family. Tiana was the chosen one.

Why?

An arm here, a leg there,
Singed to the last hair.
In the madness of their cause,
they blew us up without a pause.
We wonder why,
they chose us to die.

The Walk

Of all the Ramsay siblings, the one most attuned to the domain of spirits has always been Asha. Since childhood, she had a natural curiosity and inclination to explore the unknown. Her fascination with the paranormal overrode her fear of it.

Two activities that have always formed a part of Asha's daily routine are meditation and exercise. Regardless of where she is, she always makes time to practise both activities. It is fitting, therefore, that her birthday falls on 21st June, which is World Yoga Day.

Growing up as a Ramsay, Asha was always drawn to the charm of hill stations. The climate, the greenery and beauty of nature enraptured her over the years. Her love for the environment, be it mountain or sea, made travelling a passion.

A few years ago, Asha and her husband, Deva, along with some friends, went to Mahabaleshwar for a holiday. The picturesque resort where they were staying was located on a hillside, overlooking the Krishna River valley and the Sahyadri Hill ranges, and was bordered by a dense tropical rain forest.

After a much-needed nap post the long drive, Asha decided to go for a walk. Dressed in track pants and sneakers, she was excited and raring to work out. The weather was perfect. She breathed in the fresh air as she strolled outside the hotel gates. But after only a few steps, she paused, filled with apprehension at the blot on the landscape that greeted her.

Right across the road, overlooking the face of the hotel, was a burial ground.

What an unsuitable location to build a resort! How could this place be so highly recommended?

Casting her reservations aside, Asha resumed walking. Now that she was going to stay there for the next three days, she might as well make the most of it.

Asha increased her pace so that she could skirt the periphery of the graveyard as quickly as her legs would allow.

A crow lunged straight at her, flapping its wings threateningly. She ducked to avoid the beady-eyed bird carrying the bloody remnants of some poor creature in its shiny beak. As it flew past her, the temperate air swiftly changed into a glacial breeze, lashing against her face. Asha increased her pace. Suddenly, she felt a hard push on her back. But there wasn't a person in sight. An even harder push followed.

Who's there?

Ominous, forbidding silence. The unseen force shoved Asha again, forcing her to break into a run.

Leave me alone. Please leave me alone. I am going.

Asha's knees were going weak. She chanted her mantras continuously till she had left the cemetery far behind. Only then did the pressure propelling her forward subside. Her body belonged to her again, and the weather turned pleasant as before.

Thrown off balance by the confrontation, Asha sat on the sidewalk for a bit. After a while, she finished her walk without further altercations. On her way back, as she approached the graveyard again, she started feeling lightheaded, as tension overwhelmed her.

Stay strong. They cannot hurt you if you stay strong.

Since there was no other way to access the hotel except via the road adjacent to the graveyard, Asha braced herself. This time though, she ran back without loitering.

The next morning, she woke up early and gave in to the temptation of walking again. She had a compulsive need to stick to her routine. Her legs felt wobbly, but she steeled herself as she crossed the patch along the graveyard.

You cannot hurt me. God is with me. I am not afraid.

A crow was circling overhead menacingly. This time, it kept its distance from her.

Is it the same one?

A couple of seconds later, someone touched her. Before Asha knew what was happening, she felt her arms and body being grabbed by multiple pairs of invisible hands.

God help me!

Kicking and screaming, she tried to shake them off, but the frenzied groping would not stop. This time Asha was being pulled towards the burial ground rather than away from it.

But Asha was steadfast. *I am human! They are dust! I am not going to let them win. I am not afraid of you. I am not disturbing you. Please let me go.* Asha begged the unseen, entreating the creatures to leave her alone and managed to free herself of their tenacious grip as she charged to the other side of the road.

Asha's nature and fixation with her daily workout got the better of her yet once more, as she headed out again the following day. This time, there was a mixture of defiance and terror in her, which sent her pulse into overdrive. She kept as far away as possible from the border of the burial ground and turned her face away from it.

The biting breeze smacked her face with fervour. It tried to use its power to pull her, force her to turn her eyes towards the direction of the mute, tight-lipped graves. The muscles in her neck contracted painfully as she resisted looking at the other side.

You cannot hurt me. You cannot scare me. I trust God.

The wind gained momentum, but she used all her strength to resist its coercion. She felt like she was in the centre of a raging storm. As if possessed, the carpet of dry leaves and twigs covering the tops of the graves rose and whirled towards her. They spiralled around her frenetically, trying to lead her towards them. She prayed and continued using her energy to keep her body and face averted from the graveyard. She kept chanting *Jai Mata Di, Jai Mata Di*.

The wind disappeared as suddenly as it had appeared, and it was serene once again. Asha quickly crossed over. The cemetery seemed to have conceded defeat. The leaves fell back to the ground.

With steely determination, Asha continued on her walk. She went out every day of the holiday, adeptly manipulating her way through the unearthly obstacles thrown her way. Not even the spirits could stop her from her daily dose of exercise. The gods were on her side.

From a young girl scratched by a restless spirit to a grandmother who learned to manoeuvre her way around angry ghosts – throughout her life, Asha has ventured to places where very few people would dare to tread.

Deeply spiritual, her belief is very simple. 'There is something disturbing them, which is why they disturb us. We do not know how they died, peacefully or not. We need to help them and not be afraid of them, so they can sense our sympathy and not our fear.'

Trapped

Like caged tigers, they eternally pace.
Floating entities, with no name nor face.
They know not time nor space.
They are finished with life's endless race.

The Accident

Tiana Kirpalani, Asha Ramsay's granddaughter, has been significantly perceptive since she was young. As she has grown, her extrasensory abilities have heightened and led to eerily accurate, yet uncanny predictions.

It was Republic Day in the year 2014. Tiana, along with her father, Johnny; her sister, Sascha; paternal grandmother; and me went for lunch to a relative's house. After an afternoon well-spent, we thanked our hosts and headed back home, which was a short distance away.

I was in a rush to get home since I had made plans with some friends. Along with Tiana and Sascha, I got off at our house. My mother-in-law lived in a building close to ours, so Johnny went with her to drop her.

A few minutes after my daughters and I had entered our house, there was the sound of screeching tires, followed by a sickening thud.

A car accident.

Judging by the harsh sound of the impact, it was probably a serious one.

The girls craned their necks to look out of the window, but they could not see anything, since the house faces away from the main road. All they could see was that people were running towards the crash site.

Tiana felt her body tighten with dread. There was a painful knot in her gut.

'It's Papa!' she yelled frantically.

'What rubbish!' Sascha retorted.

'I am telling you, it is Papa! Let's go now!' Tiana insisted.

I was in the bathroom, unaware of the simmering situation outside when my mobile rang.

It was my husband. 'Listen, don't get worked up, but I have gotten into a car crash. You need to come down.'

'Are you hurt?' I could only muster those three words whilst fighting through the traumatic images of his possible injuries.

'I am fine. Don't worry. Come down immediately.'

I thought I would pass out from fear. I wanted to throw up and my legs were rubber as I went outside the room to tell the kids to come with me, but they were not around.

Where are they?

I ran out of the house, not wanting to wait a second longer. As I got out of the gate, I saw a huge crowd assembled two buildings away. I felt sick to the core as I saw a BMW angled against the divider, its front badly damaged.

If that solid car has hit our flimsy Honda City, what must have happened to Johnny!

In a trance-like state, I kept walking. I refused to allow myself to think.

Then, I saw our car. It had completely caved in on the driver's side. I thought my legs would buckle under by the time I reached it. The distance of two buildings seemed miles away as I prepared for the worst. Our car was hugging the divider; its tires had burst from the impact. The driver's side door had caved in entirely, and I saw Johnny being pulled out of it by some bystanders.

Time was moving in slow motion, and then I saw him stand upright. He seemed unhurt except for the way in which he was holding his arm.

Tiana and Sascha were rushing to his side. I ran towards them. It turned out that Johnny was fine except for a few bruises and a marginally injured shoulder. I wanted to go down on my knees and thank the Almighty for this narrow escape.

The family was visibly shaken, as we stood there viewing the damage. How unpredictable life was from one moment to another!

The way Johnny had survived was nothing short of a miracle. His car was hit twice over as he had lost control.

The BMW was careening at a 100 km/h. The rash driver had taken it out for a spin during a lunch break without the consent of his employer. He was responsible for the accident. Johnny was taking a U-turn back home, and from the corner of his eye, he had seen the BMW racing towards him at full speed. There was no place for him to swerve. Johnny had turned the car at an almost impossible angle to avoid a deadly head-on collision, and the BMW hit the side of the Honda City instead – where a few moments ago the girls and I had been sitting. We would never have survived that crash had we still been in the car.

The Honda City had swung out of control and rammed the divider, its rear hitting the BMW again whilst spinning. An unnerved Johnny sat in the car, in total shock. He looked at his reflection in the rear-view mirror.

Am I dead?

He checked himself and was amazed to find that apart from a few grazes, he had pulled through the accident without any major injury.

After the police report and other issues were sorted out, we discussed the unbelievable sequence of events. We could not get over the sheer good luck that we had been dropped off home before the calamitous crash and our gratitude at Johnny escaping from that kind of collision, more or less unscathed.

After things calmed down, I asked my daughters how they had managed to reach the accident spot even before their father had called.

Tiana simply said, 'Mom, I knew it was him. I was so sure it was him.'

In January 2017, Johnny and I were leaving for a holiday to America. On the spur of the moment, Tiana warned me, 'Take care of Papa. Watch out for what he eats and drinks.' I jokingly asked her, 'What about me?' There was no smile on Tiana's face as she repeated, 'Take care of him, Mom.' Johnny fell ill with a serious digestive disease on the holiday and had to be hospitalised. When I called up the girls to tell them of the unfortunate circumstances that had occurred, a distraught Tiana cried out, 'I knew it, Mom. I just knew it.'

Faceless

To reach out is all we wanted.
It is not you, but us who are haunted.
You cry for when we were flesh and bone.
We are still here, our souls wandering alone.

The Kittens

It is often said that the apple does not fall far from the tree. That Tiana would follow in the mystical footprints of her grandmother and mother should come as no surprise. However, considering her youth, the sheer number and range of supernatural experiences Tiana has had is staggering.

Tiana has always loved animals. It was she who came upon a litter of kittens that were born in the mezzanine of our building. Being a family of animal lovers, the girls and I took turns nurturing the five new-borns.

Unfortunately, the mother cat developed an abscess and was unable to feed them. She was sent into foster care till she healed. We could only watch helplessly as the kittens got sick one by one. Tiana tried feeding them baby food with a syringe. But the kittens kept crying piteously for their mother. Two of them passed away soon after. The third became critically ill and was so listless that I had to rush to the vet, who was unable to save it.

Seeing my daughters' tears and unable to ignore the plight of those vulnerable animals, we brought the remaining two kittens home. For the next ten days, both Tiana and Sascha took care of them, feeding them diligently and nursing them back to health. The kittens were kept in the girls' bathroom, where they were secure and undisturbed.

Things seemed to be under control when one night, the kittens' condition suddenly deteriorated.

Despite the best efforts of the family, both kittens died within hours of each other. A pall of gloom descended over the household. We had tried so hard to keep them alive. It was not fair.

For those who love animals, the death of a living creature, especially one that you have raised, is an unbearable loss. Tiana was emotionally spent with the tragic outcome and only wanted to go to bed.

The morbid silence of the room after the past few days of the feisty mewing was gnawing away at her. She switched off her mobile phone and dozed off. She was fast asleep when a glaring white light surging through the room and woke her up. She sat up in her bed, and the light grew dim.

Perplexed, she lay down again, wondering about the source of the light. Then, her mobile phone came on by itself. The screen lit up the inky blackness of the room. She picked up her phone, confused as to how it had switched itself on.

Even freakier was the detail that the screen was displaying – a message that she had sent earlier, along with a picture of the kittens. She had not touched any button on her mobile phone, so how was this even possible? Her eyes welled up with tears as she looked at the last photograph of them gazing back at her.

Wide awake by now, Tiana sat with the lights off, studying the picture of the kittens. If only she could bring them back. She so missed their mischievous yet innocent ways. When would Sascha be back home? Should she message her about the surreal goings-on? Her parents were out for dinner. Should she call them?

Then, Tiana heard it.

Miaow. Miaow.

It was the sound of the kittens' piteous mewing coming from the bathroom. Her heart skipped a beat. This was outside the realm of reality. She had personally put the bodies of the kittens into a shoebox and offered prayers as the family had put the box into the sea. A part of her did not want to enter the bathroom because it soothed her to hear the plaintive mewing, so she stayed put.

Tiana adored those kittens but was also afraid to go inside, not knowing what she might find.

After some time, the mewing stopped, and she reluctantly hauled herself into the bathroom. There was nothing there except for the residual smell the kittens had left behind. It had been a visitation, one that she perhaps sorely needed for closure. And the kittens had come back from the after-world to bid her farewell.

Despite having raised and tragically lost other pets, the kittens were the only life-form that reached out to Tiana after death. Most religions believe that all living things have a soul. It should be the natural order of things that they would have a spirit too. The animals we love as intensely as we love our children can remain dedicated to us even after their demise.

The Deep

I was often told it was a sin
But I never did listen.
I ended it all.
Further into the darkness I fall.

The Dreamer

By birth or by marriage, I do not carry the Ramsay name
— but the blood runs in my veins. I am the one who has
seen more than most. The legacy of the supernatural has
been my inheritance from my mother's side. The power
of premonition bestowed on me takes its toll, as I grapple
to comprehend the gulf between dreams and reality.

I sleep late – very late. It is often routine for me to go to bed
as the sun rises. I fill the late hours with writing to keep
myself gainfully occupied. I wish I could sleep peacefully and
without this daily toil. My mind refuses to switch off till I
have burnt it out to a point of downright exhaustion. Perhaps
my subconscious keeps me wide awake till I can bury myself
into a dreamless sleep.

In sleep, my dreams have always been vivid and often serve as re-enactments of the unpleasant thoughts that niggle at me in the day. Sometimes, I dream of the dead. Sometimes, I dream of the dying.

A long time ago, a friend of mine lost her nineteen-year-old son in a car accident. I was very fond of him and he was very fond of me. Having seen him grow up, we were devastated when he passed away suddenly and in such a tragic manner.

Over the years, I lost touch with that friend. Then one night, I dreamt of her son. We were on a terrace, and his voice was crystal clear in my head: 'Aunty, please tell Mom not to cry. I am fine.'

I woke up with a start. For the next four nights in a row, I saw the same dream, heard those same words.

I knew it would be highly insensitive to bring up my friend's son out of the blue after so many years. But I was being prodded night after night, so I had no choice but to speak with her and bring up the subject of her boy.

I called her, and we chatted for a bit. After skirting the issue for as long as I could, I took the plunge and told her that I had called because something was niggling at me, that it was to do with her son.

Initially, my friend was dumbstruck. Then, she confided in me that she had met his friend recently, and it had raked up memories. She kept visualizing what her son would have looked like had he lived to that age. My friend was sobbing while telling me about her trauma. I tried to placate her and said that I was convinced that her son was trying to communicate with her through my dreams.

'He wanted me to tell you not to cry, because he is at peace,' I finally said to her.

She was quiet for a moment and then asked me when these dreams had started. When I mentioned that they began four days ago, she was filled with amazement.

'I met his friend exactly four days ago. You chose to get in touch after so long. This cannot be a coincidence, can it? And how would you even know I have been crying?' she asked wondrously.

I was stunned.

'I had no idea, but he was aware of what you were going through. Try and be happy for his sake. That's all he wants.' As I spoke, I knew what I had said was true.

I had done what I was asked to do. When I put down the phone, I felt at ease and so did my friend.

The dreams stopped after that call.

My closest friend was having a harrowing time with her mother's cancer. Life has been far from easy for her, and she was tasked with being the caregiver to other ailing family members as well. When her ill mother, who was a wonderful and resilient person, visited Mumbai, I went over to meet her.

'I am truly glad my daughter has a friend like you,' she told me. 'I know you will be there for her when I am not around.'

The simple faith her mother had invested in me was touching. 'Don't worry, Aunty. I will always be there for her. You get better.'

I hugged her mother tight, even though this was the first time I was meeting her. Some people have such a positive aura that you connect with them instantly. She was one such pure soul.

My friend lived in Mumbai while her mother lived in Delhi. So, the friend had to travel back and forth for her treatment. On one such occasion, when she was back in Mumbai, I was in Goa on a holiday.

Usually on a vacation, I cut off from everything back home and relax. I was having an afternoon siesta, as I often do on holidays, when I was roused awake. I had dreamt of my friend's mother. This had never happened before.

In my dream, I could only recall her face and her trying to tell me something. It was like she was levitating through space, struggling to reach me.

I immediately messaged my friend to enquire about her mother's health. There was no response till much later. She replied asking why I had asked her that out of the blue since I was on holiday. I told her about my dream. She was speechless and what she told me afterwards struck me like a bolt of lightning.

'At the precise time you messaged me, my aunt in Delhi was trying to wake up my mother. But she was not responding. She is a light sleeper, so obviously we got worried. Then abruptly she woke up, but was disoriented. Though I did not reply to your message at that time, I thought it very odd that you asked about her in that instant. Why would you dream about her?'

I told my astounded friend about the promise I had made to her mother.

I firmly believe that in that duration of unresponsiveness, Aunty had tried to connect with me to remind me to be there for her daughter. She had beaten all odds to survive for seven years with advanced cancer. The doctors used to call her a walking miracle.

Spurred by that amazing resolve, she chose to hang on for her daughter's sake and came back that day. It was not her time yet.

Unfortunately, Death is always the merciless victor in life's warfare. I was lucky enough to meet Aunty again in her last days, before she passed away in August 2019. In the hospital, I reassured her about our undisclosed pact. She smiled gratefully as she kissed my hand through the forbidding, hard plastic of the breathing mask that separated us.

There are many instances when I have guessed someone's physical illness or precarious state of mind, sometimes even before they have been privy to it. It just stares me in the face, and I feel duty bound to communicate it to them. The reactions are not always favourable. At times, I am even subjected to ridicule. But that is the price I have to pay for my unyielding belief. I keep reminding myself that it is not about me, but for them.

A tingle in my limbs when I am in a room full of people, and I can pick up sadness exuding from an unknown source. An overpowering need to warn someone when I have a hunch that there is a crisis on the horizon. My premonitions are not a daily occurrence, but when they happen, I act on them. As far as people go, I am plagued 24x7 by heightened sensitivity to their mannerisms, moods and masks. I am drawn to honesty and respectful of the vulnerability of being human that often accompanies truth.

People who are manipulative, envious and self-serving trigger warning bells in my head. I feel sapped in their presence and in the negativity of their aura. Sooner or later, they leave my life. Either I remove them, or they are yanked away. It's a purposeful purging that proves itself over time. Through trial by fire, I have learnt one thing: to trust my intuition. I have been right way more often than I have been wrong.

One More Breath

We left life behind
Yet happiness we do not find.
Give us one more breath
So we can rewrite our death.

Jakarta

Over the years, I have learnt that spirits have no geographical divisions. They are everywhere, and we carry within us the ability to connect with them.

My sister-in-law lives in Jakarta. Indonesia, like India, is a land that lays pronounced emphasis on rituals and religion. It is a predominantly Muslim country. Jakarta is a very crowded metropolis and Indonesia's most advanced city.

It was August 2018. My sister-in-law's birthday was coming up, and she was very eager to have all of us by her side to celebrate the momentous day. The family is spread all over the world, from Canada to Dubai, but we wanted to be together for her birthday celebrations.

She and her husband live in a four-bedroom bungalow and usually we stay with them when we visit Jakarta. But this time around, their home was packed with houseguests, so they graciously offered us the use of an apartment close to their residence.

My husband and I arrived at their house at 8 p.m., and after chatting with the family until midnight, we went to our apartment. Though we could not see much at that time of the night, it seemed to be an agreeable residential building. The apartment was a spacious two-bedroom unit. It had been a gruelling journey from Mumbai to Jakarta, so we decided to get in a decent night's sleep before the festivities of the next day.

Johnny fell asleep almost immediately. I lounged in bed, eyes wide open as I usually do at night, tossing and turning, more so because it was an unfamiliar place and the air-conditioner made an irritating hum.

As I waited for sleep to come, I suddenly felt a heaviness in the room. There was an uneasiness building in my head. I was ready to fall asleep, but my mind would not shut down. There was a haze of light coming through the curtains. It added to my inability to fall asleep.

Annoyed, I turned away from the light to the other side of the bed to come face-to-face with the scariest sight of my life.

There was a man towering over me. Less of a man and more of a shadow. He was extraordinarily tall and was peering at me. He said nothing, did nothing, except study me.

I was too afraid to turn on my back to wake up my husband. I was too afraid to shout. The palpitations of my heart were so loud, I could hear them.

Is this real or is my weary mind playing a trick on me?

I vaulted over and switched on the bedside lamp. The shadowy man dissipated into nothingness.

Am I delirious? Had I fallen asleep?

No ... I was sure that my unwelcome guest was an actual ghost.

By now, I was fully awake. Sleep was the last thing on my mind, so I decided to go to the hall. By now, it was almost 4 a.m. I was worn out, but the house seemed to be laden with an overhanging denseness, which was suffocating me.

I went out to the balcony, thinking the fresh air would help. But when I looked down, I almost fainted in fear. Never had I seen anything like this.

Tucked away beside a busy highway, fenced in by high-rise buildings, in the heart of the city, was the most humongous graveyard I have ever laid eyes on. Glistening in the dark, lit up by the moonlight, were hundreds of graves. The graveyard was at least a kilometre long and wide.

I hastened back into the room, falling over my feet.

Back in the bedroom, I peeked out of the curtained window and noticed there were graves after graves there, neatly arranged in innumerable rows. Coffins and tombstones enclosed the circumference of the building, with only a wall dividing us.

I jostled my husband out of his slumber and told him all that had happened. On my insistence, he looked out of the window and let out a low whistle at the army of crypts. The one thing he has learnt over the years is to not take me lightly when it comes to things like these.

It was too late to go anywhere else, so I suggested that he go back to sleep but we leave first thing next morning.

The hubbub of cars racing by on the highway was very disruptive, so he used earplugs to shut out the never-ending buzz. As for me, I was too frazzled to sleep. I sat in vigil, on my guard, waiting for sunrise.

When would this night end?

The neighbouring mosque blared prayers on the loudspeaker, and it was comforting to hear them. I imagined the prayers to be a lullaby for the dead to repose and for the morning to make its way to the living.

After what felt like forever, dawn broke. I went out to the balcony to see the cemetery again. It was even larger than I had earlier surmised. Yet, it seemed less frightening in sunlight. There were tombs and tombstones of assorted sizes, colours and shapes, though white was the predominant colour.

I wanted to leave as soon as possible. The house still felt claustrophobic and was stifling me.

I washed my face and came out of the bathroom to find my husband searching the room. He was not able to find one of his earplugs. He had looked everywhere – on the bed, under it, on the bedside, but could not find it. He helped me pack and kept speculating about where it could have been mislaid.

Then he saw it, right under his nose, on the bed that he had checked thoroughly a few minutes earlier.

Lying on the pristine white bed-sheet, sticking out like a sore thumb, was the missing bright orange earplug. We were truly confused because both of us had checked that area twice already, and it was not there.

How was it possible that such a colourful earplug was nowhere to be found and then suddenly turned up by itself right under his nose?

Both of us looked at each other, not needing to say a thing. He glanced out of the window, now fully awake and shook his head in disbelief.

'Let's get the hell out of here right now!' he said.

And, so we did.

It was awkward to explain to my sister-in-law and her husband why we did not want to stay in the apartment. I blamed it on the mattress, saying that it was aggravating my cervical spondylitis issue. Whilst chatting, they told us how they always had full occupancy while leasing the apartment, taking into account the central location. It had always fetched a good return on the investment. I idly speculated to myself about how many of those tenants and residents in that building now believed in ghosts. Was any price worth finding out?

The Warrior

I do not accept death.
I will fight even after my last breath.
I have nothing left to lose.
No fear of knife or noose.

King Kripps

My husband's brother, Rajan Kirpalani, passed away in September 2015 after a spirited tussle with cancer. He was only fifty-five years old and left behind four beautiful children, a devoted wife and a grieving family. He lived as he died, a powerful decision-maker till the end, like his favourite song – Frank Sinatra's 'My Way'.

Near and dear ones affectionately called my brother-in-law Rajan, Raju. We met at Cellars, a discotheque at the Oberoi Hotel. Cellars was a hotspot for most people in the disco era of 1980s Bombay.

I was a 19-year-old girl back then, and it was my first time visiting this very popular nightspot. Imagine my excitement when this handsome stranger asked me to dance. We spent the night dancing and chatting nineteen to a dozen. I would never have envisaged what destiny had in store.

The next time I went to Cellars, I saw the stranger again. I went over to say hello and he looked at me blankly as if he did not recognize me at all. The conversation is still etched in my memory as though it happened yesterday.

'Hi!'

'Do we know each other?'

'We danced the other night?'

'I am sorry, I don't think I have ever met you.'

'Oh.'

'Listen, are you mistaking me for Rajan?'

'You are not Rajan?'

'No, I am his brother, Johnny.'

That is how I met my husband. I mistook him for his brother. Yes, they looked *very* similar. And after only one meeting in a poorly lit nightclub, could anyone blame me for making the best mistake of my life?

Six years later, Johnny and I were married. The year was 1992. We even had a double wedding – Rajan and Millie, along with Johnny and I.

It was a fairy tale for almost two decades. Outings full of chitchat, family dinners and late night coffee. Though we lived in different homes, the four of us spent a considerable amount of time together.

Raju and I were less in-laws and more buddies. There was a mischievous glint in his eyes whenever he saw me. I was the butt of most of his pranks, and we were invariably engaged in trying to outdo the other in quick-witted banter. Those were merry times, till Raju fell ill with chronic pancreatitis.

He was in and out of hospital and in terrible pain most of the time. The illness took a toll on him and his capacity to be the light-hearted man we knew. Distance crept in, and we drifted apart for a while.

One day, I told my husband that we should meet Raju more often than we did. His lifestyle deterioration with pancreatitis was on-going but a nagging dread had started bugging me, and I could not place my finger on it.

Sure enough, Raju's health issues started to worsen soon after. The doctors thought he had developed diverticulitis, based on the initial tests they conducted, but my gut feeling warned me that there was more. I was convinced he had cancer, before he or the doctors even suspected it. I voiced my angst to my husband, who assured me they would find out what was wrong with Raju but that nothing seemed alarming yet.

Unfortunately, I was right. It turned out to be colon cancer. To say the diagnosis torpedoed all of us would be an understatement. Raju knew his days were numbered, and his only wish was to spend as much time with his family as possible. The doctors had given him three months to a year to live. He only got three weeks.

A fortnight before he passed away, I had the cherished opportunity to speak to him privately. His stoic deference to his hopeless situation was admirable. It was the most lionhearted attitude I have witnessed in my entire life. It inspired me to write a short story – of his tribulation, of his dignity and of his strength. I finished the story at 5 a.m. on 29 September 2015. He passed away the same day, around 10 a.m. He never got a chance to read it.

As his body lay in the room, waiting for cremation, the living room was filling up with friends and family. Raju's son, Rushil, with whom I share a very special bond, came up to me, touched my feet out of respect, and said, 'Dad says he's sorry.'

I was taken aback, so I asked him what he meant. He looked me straight in the eye and cryptically said, 'You know.'

In his remaining time, my brother-in-law in a beautiful gesture had asked forgiveness of almost everyone he might have inadvertently hurt in his lifetime. He never got the opportunity to tell me so. This must have been the only way, through his son, who is so dear to me.

One can never be prepared for the death of a loved one, even with the excruciating advance notice. It rips your insides with its pitiless finality. Such is the nature of loss.

Later that night, I was by myself in my own house, flashbacks of the past running through my anguished mind. I perceived the presence of someone near the main door. Every instinct told me it was Raju. I turned to look, but there was nobody. I would have brushed it off as the overwhelming impact of grief, but for my pet cat, Buzz.

Buzz's eyes were fixed on the door, his body arched in high alert, looking at exactly the same spot where I was conscious of Raju's presence.

All I could think of was Raju's words to me in his final days, 'When was the last time you invited us over?'

He had come over.

The next morning, after a night of fragmented sleep, I switched on my phone. All the photographs and messages from the time he had told us that he had a few months to live right up to his death were missing from my phone.

It was as if the most painful stage of the cancer he must have endured in those last three weeks had been erased from my mobile. I have no digital memory of that time on my phone except for his obituary, which was the only trace left of him or of that month in 2015.

Then, there was the time I walked into the hall from my children's room. I caught a glimpse of my husband. As I called out, the person disappeared from my sight almost instantly. On hearing me call his name, my husband came out from our bedroom. Befuddled, it soon dawned on me that it was Raju I had seen. The physical similarity between my husband and him had confused me yet again. It all happened in a flash, but I know it was him.

Raju was a very stylish dresser. He wore the quirkiest colours, from yellow to electric blue. He could carry off burgundy trousers and matching moccasins with a flourish.

After his demise, my daughter, Tiana, was sitting in my in-law's house and chatting with her sister, Sascha. It was around 3 a.m. In the glass of the window Tiana was facing, she saw the reflection of someone walking behind her. He was wearing burgundy trousers. She was so startled that she almost fell off her chair. There was nobody behind her, but she suspected at once that it was the spirit of her late uncle walking through the house.

Raju loved being with family. His last wish was for us not to converse about his illness but simply to spend time with him, doing the things we enjoyed together. I strongly believe he misses us just as much as we miss him, so he is trying to forge a connection. His premature death was a cruel joke played by destiny. Perhaps, he is trying to scare the life out of me, and I can imagine his infectious and effusive laughter at pulling off yet another prank at my expense, this time from the great beyond. As for me, I have run out of repartees. There is only stagnant and cadaverous silence.

In January 2017, Johnny and I went to Miami for our 25th anniversary. A day after landing in America, we boarded a ship for a Caribbean cruise. Hours later, my husband fell ill onboard. We were disembarked, and he was taken straight to the hospital. Johnny was diagnosed with an attack of acute pancreatitis, exactly like his brother. He had never had any signs of the disease previously. The only reason he received timely help for this was because we were familiar with the symptoms due to Raju's unfortunate duel with pancreatitis. If this had happened one day earlier, we would have been airborne; one day later, and we would have been at sea, with no access to the emergency medical aid he needed. In this tragic twist of fate, we had to count our blessings that we had seen the ugly face of this illness at close quarters through Raju, which gave Johnny a fighting chance.

I had received signals of the imminent danger, but I was not evolved enough to read the signs. There was a photograph of the two of us in the bedroom, in which only Johnny's face was damaged by moisture while mine was flawless. I found that baffling but disregarded it. Before taking off for the cruise, goaded by my children's persistence, Johnny proposed to me all over again with them in attendance. That particular photograph, where I wore the anniversary ring that he had gifted me was blurred, like an omen of impending disaster. The camera never lies, and we were being cautioned.

Many a palm reader has commented on the significance of the trident on my hand being on my heart line. In the second year of our marriage, when my daughter, Sascha, was three months old, we went to Phuket. Johnny had a parasailing accident and broke his knee. Bringing him back home was riddled with obstacles, but after much difficulty, I managed to get him to Bombay a week later, where he had a surgery. I have never fully recovered from the trauma of having a tiny baby and dealing with the repercussions of his accident by myself in a foreign land. Who would have thought I would be in that same position twenty-five years later? The palm readers were accurate. I am meant to protect the man I love.

Along with me, perhaps Raju is his brother's keeper, his bodyguard in heaven, and that faith keeps me going day after day.

The Protector

For you, they stay,
each night and each day.
They watch while you sleep,
A promise they must keep.

The Guardian Angel

Kalawanti Thawani was my paternal grandmother. Everyone called her 'Bhabhi', as did I. The events of this story led me to accept the fact that I had the gift, or the curse, of premonition. The belief in spirits began during this period in my life and has only increased with time and with many other occurrences.

I lived in a large joint family at Marine Drive, along with my grandparents, parents, siblings, uncle and four aunts till they got married. I was the first-born child of the first-born son of the house, a position I did not enjoy. Along with the attention came an excess of accountability. As a young girl, I used to think that my grandmother, Bhabhi, kept too watchful an eye on me. She would report everything to my grandfather, who was an authoritarian.

Bhabhi was a short, wheat-complexioned lady, with a thin ponytail. She wore saris and her glasses were always perched on her small face. She watched everything on television, so despite her lack of formal education, she could rattle off cricket scores and confer about political scandals.

I can still taste the delicious potato dish she made for me at any unreasonable hour, whenever I felt hungry. I regret that though I was fond of her, the family and I never wholly expressed the love that she craved for from everyone. We took her for granted.

Since Bhabhi was a homebody, she was privy to the goings-on in my life, and I found her concern and advice intrusive and annoying. *The folly of youth.* To put it bluntly, I was a typical, self-absorbed youngster with minimal sensitivity towards the emotional needs of other family members.

I was married on 31 January 1992. Bhabhi was ecstatic to see me as a bride, partaking in all the wedding ceremonies with unbridled enthusiasm. She had always had a special affection for my husband, Johnny, and had showered him with affection throughout our long engagement.

In May 1992, I was visiting my family home. Out of the blue, Bhabhi asked me if I was expecting. I burst into laughter, telling her I had no intention of having children in the near future. I had been married a little over three months and wanted to enjoy life for the moment.

But Bhabhi insisted that I was expecting.

A month later, I discovered that I was indeed pregnant, despite all the necessary precautions. I was shocked, to put it mildly. *How did Bhabhi know that before I did?*

But I did not dwell on the thought for too long, because we were too busy trying to figure out the best way to deliver the news to our families.

I distinctly remember the conversation with my husband like it was yesterday. 'Why don't you tell them on your mother's birthday? It will make it even more special,' he suggested.

I was less inclined towards this plan.

My mother's birthday was right around the corner, on the 21st of June, and Bhabhi was going for a cataract surgery on the 19th of June.

'Who knows about life?' I blurted out. 'Why wait? I want to tell my grandmother before the cataract procedure.'

Soon after, I told Bhabhi sheepishly that I was expecting – just like she had said. Her knowing smile is still carved in my mind. She was beaming from ear to ear as she hugged me. I kept asking her how she knew about the pregnancy. But she refused to answer and only smiled enigmatically.

The next day, Bhabhi went for the cataract surgery. During the procedure, she had a massive heart attack.

The ophthalmologist had assumed that she was riddled with severe anxiety and had ignored her complaints of chest pain. On the insistence of the family, an electrocardiogram was conducted, and she was immediately admitted to the hospital.

Bhabhi held on for a total of three days after that and floated in and out of consciousness. Her younger son, a cardiologist, was in America and flew back urgently. Shortly after seeing him, her body succumbed to another heart attack, and she passed away on 22 June 1992. She was sixty-seven years old.

Who knows about life?

Those accursed words. Why had they even crossed my mind? And why did they have to come true? If I had decided to give her the news of my pregnancy on my mother's birthday, she would not have been conscious enough to register them.

As the family sponged her body to prepare her for the funeral, I watched her limp form in a daze. The image of the scanty strands of hair sticking to the back of her lolling neck haunts me even now.

According to Hindu customs, it is unlucky for an expecting woman to be in proximity to a corpse. But I refused to listen to anyone and was present through all the final rites. I embraced my grandmother for the last time and placed her hand on my stomach, asking for her blessings.

I felt as though Bhabhi had breathed life into my womb, so she could see me settled and secure before she left her earthly body. After all, it was she who had lifted and wrapped me in her sari when my mother gave birth to me in the car. She had held me all the way to the hospital, where the doctor severed the umbilical cord at the emergency entrance.

My welcome into this world had been in her arms.

The night she died, I was overcome with grief. My husband had dozed off, but sleep eluded me. The upsetting visual of Bhabhi's body was stuck in my head.

Tears were pouring down my face and I was racked with sobs.

The room was exceptionally chilly, and the air-conditioner was giving me uncontrollable tremors. Simultaneously, I was hit by a blast of bitterly cold air. The bathroom door banged open and shut by itself repeatedly. I tried to wake up Johnny, but he did not stir.

The racket stopped and a curious sensation – like a soft current of velvet – swept over me. I felt a sense of serenity engulf me, and immediately, I fell into soothing slumber.

The incident was as real as my wretched intuition had proven to be.

Around the fifth month of my pregnancy, I developed complications. The amniotic fluid began to leak, and my baby was given a one per cent chance of survival. I was put on bed rest in the hope that it would stop the problem, or at least delay the inevitable, to buy valuable time. My parents visited me every day for the ten days that I was hospitalized, except for the day they went to the temple to perform a ceremony, offering prayers for Bhabhi.

It had been three months since her demise. When I heard where they had been, I felt a curious boost of confidence surging through me.

'This baby will survive. I know it. Bhabhi is watching over her.'

The amniotic fluid leak stopped that day itself, and I was discharged soon after. The doctors were amazed at the turn of events because nobody had expected a positive outcome. Though the situation improved, it was still a very risky pregnancy, so I spent the full trimester taking it easy in bed. But unyielding faith had built up in me over this time, a courage that came from conviction. *We were going to make it!*

Sascha was born on 16 February 1993 – a beautiful, healthy, baby girl.

My miracle baby. My gift from my grandmother.

> *'Don't grieve. Anything you lose comes round in*
> *another form.'*
> —*Rumi*

The worst phase of my adult life so far started in 2012 and has gone on for an extended period of time. I sought answers from every avenue I could – temples to talismans. A renowned medium, who communicates with the dead, asked for photographs of family and friends to see if there were any negative influences in my life. He further told me there was an elderly lady protecting me and inquired if someone very dear to me had expired. As he flipped through the photographs of the people in the album, he pointed to a specific one and identified her as my guardian angel, the one who was looking out for me. It was Bhabhi!

Imprisonment

Being here is not my choice.
I scream, but I have no voice.
Please listen to my plight.
Release me to the white light.
I really want to go
to that heavenly glow.

The Hand of God

Of all the encounters I have narrated in this book, none has affected me as much as the one that follows. It is only befitting that this be the final story, since it triggered my quest into the world beyond the one we know.

For as far back as I can remember, I have been told that I have a black tongue. My premonitions stupefy me. They hound me with bullying clarity. It was not long before people outside my family started noticing it too.

Predictions that involuntarily slipped out of my mouth would sooner or later be proven true. For me, it has always been a balancing act between understanding the difference between worry and intuition, especially when it comes to my immediate family. A huge blind-spot blocks my sixth sense when it involves my family, which perhaps preserves my sanity.

Every summer, my husband, Johnny; my daughters, Sascha and Tiana; and I go for a family holiday. In 2012, I expressed a desire to go to Spain, which had always been on top of my bucket list.

Unplanned, the statement rolled off my tongue: 'I want to go see Spain now, because I have a feeling life is going to change forever.'

Johnny looked at me curiously but decided to go along with the suggestion. A vacation was the cherry on the icing of our world. We were already blessed with amazing friends, family and a marvellous manner of living filled with health and harmony.

We planned to visit Turkey and Spain and to go on a Mediterranean cruise. I wanted to save Barcelona for the end, because it seemed like the perfect city with which to conclude the vacation.

I ticked off many places on my wish-list – Istanbul, Rome, Florence, Madrid, Ibiza, the French Riviera. I absolutely loved cruising to every single one of those places. It was a thrilling trip, and each city was an adventure in itself.

When we reached Barcelona, our final destination, it was vibrant and exciting – everything that I had expected and more! I had chalked out a detailed itinerary for each day and could not wait to explore the city.

27 May 2012.

I remember the date vividly. It is time stamped on every photograph and recollection. We set out to visit the tourist attractions of Barcelona. Sagrada Familia, Barcelona's most famous church, was to be the grand finale of our sightseeing itinerary that day. The brilliant architect Antoni Gaudi had devoted more than forty years to its construction. An eminently religious man, Gaudi had surrendered the last twelve years of his life to the service of God through his craft. The church is his unfinished masterpiece and has been under construction since 1882, more than a century in the making. It is expected to be completed in 2026.

We chose to visit the Nativity Facade because it was built by Gaudi and was rich in architectural detail, compared to rather plain Passion facade. There is a bridge connecting two of the towers, and the view from there is supposed to be incredible.

The use of the elevator was only allowed for going up, so one has to walk down from the towers using a steep, winding staircase. But due to a previous ligament tear in my ankle, I was granted permission to use the elevator on the way down as well.

After enjoying the magnificent view of Barcelona from the bridge, my husband and children started walking down the stairs of the tower. I headed to the other side, towards the elevator. I was the only person headed in that direction, since everybody else was climbing down. Captivated by the medieval stonewalls and the narrow, curving passages, I began filming my walk.

I stood at the top of a short flight of stairs, video camera in hand and the elevator a few steps away. There was an open window on the right side and an impenetrable stone wall to the left. I ran my fingers over the ridges of the wall, impressed with their ability to stand the test of time. They had withstood the ravages of history, and it felt sublime to be by myself and absorb the atmosphere.

I continued filming on my way down, slowly walking down the archaic stone steps and then through my lens, I saw the most astonishing sight.

Right in front of me was what looked like a white translucent hand, its fingers diaphanous as it made its way from the thick wall. It looked almost anaemic, as if the blood in its non-existent arteries had been savagely depleted.

I fell back, almost dropping my camera in the process. Steadying myself, I clambered back to the top step.

What on earth was that?

Examining the layout, I deduced that it could not be a reflection or a trick of sunlight, because it had come from the solid wall. I gingerly stepped down the stairs again, my camera on. And there it was again, advancing in that slow-moving motion. It was a see-through hand, as fine as gauze, the outline of its fingers distinct. It progressed from the wall towards the window. There seemed to be nothing malevolent about it, but I was flustered nonetheless.

I had never seen anything remotely like that, except in scary movies. Panic stricken, I sprinted down the remaining few steps and got into the empty elevator.

Seeing my husband and daughters, I excitedly told them that I had encountered a spirit. They thought I was imagining things till I showed them the video I had shot.

There it was, alive on the screen, those ghostly fingers bit by bit blocking my path.

It seemed to be trying to stop me from going ahead.

My husband reluctantly acknowledged that it did look like a hand. I assured my children that it must be a blessing in disguise. Somehow, I was not afraid – not then, not later. It did not seem evil, or maybe the fact that we were in a church just made it seem less frightening and more divine.

I would soon find out what was lying in wait for us.

We reached the hotel, and I started feeling extremely cold, like I had icicles in the very core of my bones. My body started twitching. and despite all the thick blankets my family used to cover me, the shivering did not stop for quite a while.

I did not associate the happenings at Sagrada Familia with my condition. I blamed it on the debilitating after-effect of an extensive day of sightseeing. The holiday was pretty uneventful after that, and we reached India in one piece.

In June 2012, around a fortnight after landing back in Mumbai, I had a series of seizures. In the middle of the night, my body began to thrash brutally and repeatedly. My husband, unsure of how to handle me, held me down with as much strength as he could.

In that state of semi-consciousness, I hurt my shoulder, my head and even my husband. It was as if something had taken possession of my mind and was punishing my body. Just when we thought it was over, another bout of convulsions would begin.

An ambulance was called, and I was rushed to the hospital. I was admitted to the Intensive Care Unit. After running a battery of tests, they could not find anything wrong, so they diagnosed me with Psychological Non Epileptic Seizures, caused by severe anxiety and precipitated by menopause. I was prescribed anti-epileptics and anti-anxiety drugs. The doctor ordered me to take it easy and reduce the stress factors in my life.

Ironically, life decided to test my limits.

A month later, in July 2012, my daughter, Tiana, developed a low-grade fever and a cough that would just not stop. She was fifteen-years-old at the time. By the end of the year, she had been to hospital four times. Finally, they did an exploratory laparoscopic surgery and detected a handful of mercifully minor issues, which they soon sorted.

For the next few years, however, Tiana's health complications persisted. She was constantly afflicted by a hacking cough and breathing difficulties. Between 2012 and 2018, she had been admitted to the hospital seven times, notwithstanding the countless visits to doctors and nightly emergency trips to the casualty ward.

It was a bubbling cauldron of unyielding pressure on my family – between her ceaseless health problems and my frequent seizures. I had reached the end of my tether and began looking for answers surpassing science and medicine.

In the thick of the problems afflicting us, I met a renowned 'coffee cup reader' at a friend's son's wedding. After the guests had dwindled away, I approached the lady. Studying the formation in her cup, she looked at me unflinchingly and said, 'I stayed longer to meet you. It is clobbering you, isn't it? It is hurting you through the one you really love. What a fight you have put up! Keep fighting back, and it will ultimately leave you be. I admire your strength!'

What strength? I thought to myself. I had never felt weaker. I wanted to break down and cry. My suspicions had been correct. There was an unholy presence badgering us. The lady had conveyed all this without me asking her a single question about my situation. The church occurrence had launched us into this nightmare, and I no longer thought of it as a celestial happening.

Soon, my seizures increased to two to three times a week. They would start the same way. I would feel this rising iciness in my feet that would spread through my body, and then I would be bludgeoned by uncontrollable convulsions. To say that it was a distressing period would be an understatement.

It was during this time that we came across a famous medium, one who could communicate with the dead through auto-writing. Johnny and the medium had been acquaintances back in the day. As the two exchanged pleasantries, while the medium looked at me keenly. 'You are a receiver, aren't you? You can communicate with the dead. Develop your gift.'

I was flabbergasted and desperately resolved to meet with him again. I fixed an appointment in the hope of getting some answers for the avalanche of troubles that was bombarding our lives. I showed him the Sagrada Familia video, and he told me what I had encountered was a harmless astral spirit, but there were other negative influences eroding our existence. He said that I was protected by my paternal grandmother, Bhabhi, whom he had identified through the photographs I had brought with me. He was very accurate about the negative people around us and asked us to keep away from them. He assured me that my daughter and I would be fine, but we had cause for concern about someone else in the family.

'It is him that you have to worry about,' he said, pointing to Johnny.

I glanced at my husband, and then willed myself into denial. We were so relieved to hear that we were going to survive this ordeal that we focused on that optimism. Neither of us could deal with any more stress, so we glossed over the warning about Johnny.

But the medium was right!

In 2013, Johnny lost his father. The year after that, he got into a car crash but miraculously survived. In 2015, he lost his brother. Two years later, he was diagnosed with pancreatitis. Through all this, he was dealing with a wife besieged by seizures, one daughter constantly in and out of hospitals, and another daughter perennially in pain since she had developed endometriosis and a stubborn ovarian cyst.

I was feuding with my own demons alongside. In 2014, I had a fall and tore the ligaments in one foot. In 2015, I fractured my toe. In 2016, my father was diagnosed with a critical illness. In 2017, I suffered from cervical slipped disc. In 2018, I developed hypertension, and in 2019, I broke my finger. In 2020, Tiana contracted COVID-19 while studying in London and was stranded there, alone and recurrently ill.

Back then, in a bid for stability, I let go of a few relationships, including my oldest and closest friend. For me, friendship has always been about loyalty and unconditional support. And I was completely disillusioned with the lack of empathy towards our situation and the appalling shallowness of our equation. I could not handle any more grief, betrayal or pressure, neither from friend nor from family.

Considering all that we had lost, I did not want to lose my mind totally too. I had nothing more left to give to the habitual takers. The ruthless insensitivity of some was too great to ignore. A couple of blood ties were washed away in the tempest, just like drain water. The flimsy bridges had to be burned so there would be no burden of expectation. It hurt like hell. But it had to be done. I had no bandwidth for discordant people.

It is often said, that when it rains, it pours. During this time, there were bolts of bad luck hurled at us on the professional front too. One adversity after another was chasing at our heels, and nothing was working out for us.

On the advice of the medium, I lit glass lamps in my house to absorb negativity. The glasses would crack almost every other day. The oil would be black, or the wicks would be floating upside down. We could not find any logical answers to these occurrences, so we took solace in the supposition that they were doing their job of protecting us.

During the peak of Tiana's illness, I lit a few lamps in her room and perched them on her study desk. One day, she was sitting on a chair near her desk when all the lamps started crackling. The lights of the wicks flickered madly. Right before us, the total lot of glasses cracked one by one, in a straight sequence. Some shattered into pieces while we watched. It was absolutely terrifying.

Who or what were we up against?

I spent time prostrate in prayer, begging the gods to have mercy and stop this onslaught. Other times, I challenged the malicious entity that I would not let it hurt my girls or my husband.

It took a lot of courage, as an individual and as a family, to go through this trying spell.

Lately, the seizures have diminished in regularity and now barely seem to surface. My children are getting their lives together. We are all limping back to some semblance of normalcy. We have made it till here, bruised and battered but alive.

Up to this time I feel there is an ongoing battle between good and evil looming over me. A missile is thrown at me and then correspondingly a hidden reserve of strength arises and combats it. Is it God, goddess or grandmother that is shielding us from this ferocious onslaught? Whatever is attacking us, something greater is protecting us. I maintain this.

My mother was instrumental in putting things in perspective with her no-frills wisdom. 'For 20 years you hardly had any complaints about life. The way you accepted that prosperity, you have to accept these adversities too. Life always balances itself out.'

It was undeniably tough, to say the least. Looking back, it was strangely enlightening too. In these recent years, I have lost a lot, but I have gained much too. I have gained faith that I am divinely protected. I have raised my levels of acceptance, empathy and gratitude.

I was pushed to find myself in this chaos and wrote my first novel, *Out With Lanterns*. I am writing this book you hold in your hands, only because I was forced to delve deeper to find answers. I am a stronger and more spiritual person today. I survived. We survived. We are blessed.

My husband wanted the video of the hand from Sagrada Familia erased from every device in our house. He is of the opinion that it is the root cause of the reversal of fortune that had come our way.

I have lived those seconds at the church, time and time again, in my head. Was it the hand of God I saw, a heavenly forewarning of the turbulent times ahead? Or, was it an evil force that attached itself to me and ravaged our lives?

Either way, I got rid of the video from all the equipment at home upon my husband's request. I have it stored away in an autonomous email box, imprisoned in cyberspace. It's my only concrete proof of an unknown world.

I have never looked at the recording again, but I know it holds a cryptic secret of the universe.

I have never looked at the recording again.

Is it even conceivable that an ordinary person like me could hold an extraordinary, cryptic secret of the universe? Who am I to think that I could possibly have the elusive answer to the ultimate enigma: Do ghosts exist?

Who am I?

Since 2012, I have repeatedly seen the number '33' everywhere. On a car ahead of me, in a movie, on a table reservation. The Honda City registered in my name that bore the brunt of my husband's accident and was instrumental in his providential escape had the licence plate number '3301'. I did some research and learnt that 33 is a very significant number. To my amazement, I discovered something else too, but much later. Jesus Christ's age was 33 at the time of his crucifixion and resurrection. On the Passion facade of Sagrada Familia is a 4 x 4 magic square, whose numbers in rows, columns or diagonal lines always add up to 33.

Eternity

Our first breath
brings us one step closer to death.
From that birth cry
to that final goodbye,
the inevitable is undeniable to see,
yet we desperately seek immortality.

Afterword

As the embodied soul continually passes, in this body, from boyhood to youth to old age, the soul similarly passes into another body at death. The self-realized soul is not bewildered by such a change.

—*Bhagavad Gita 2.13*

O soul thou that art at rest, return to thy Lord, well-pleased, well pleasing, so enter among My servants, and enter My Garden.

—*The Holy Quran 89:27-30*

The living know that they will die; but the dead know nothing, and they have no more reward, for the memory of them is forgotten. Also their love, their hatred, and their envy have now perished; nevermore will they have a share in anything done under the sun.

—*Ecclesiastes 9:5 ESV*

When I decided to write this book, I knew that I would be risking my credibility as a person. People would think I had lost my mind or that I was exploiting my position as a Ramsay family member. But this did not stop me, because I was clear about my intent to tell these stories as honestly and sincerely as I could.

My purpose is to create hope, not fear – hope that those that have passed away continue to exist in a realm that may be out of our reach but closer to us than we realize. Perhaps that thought could provide comfort to the bereaved, who are battling the heart-wrenching pain of losing a beloved one. Seeing us in anguish while we lament their loss must tear apart their souls of the deceased, who can only look on helplessly. They can neither wipe our tears nor their own. However lonely as we feel, the spirits must feel it tenfold. So we must heal – for our sakes as much as theirs.

Death cannot be allowed to triumph over the human spirit or over the power of love. In writing this book, I call forth the bravery within us, to bounce back from the sledgehammer blows rained on us by the tyranny of death.

I write for the souls that have found peace and for those that are still wandering, seeking absolution. As among humans, there are good as well as evil spirits. To the benign spirits that crave our attention, we must offer understanding, endorsement and compassion. Against a hostile spirit, we must stay positive, keep faith and garner spiritual strength. Most of all, we must believe that for every devil, there is a guardian angel. The Almighty gifts us his divine protection through the souls of those who have left us but will always love us.

Perhaps, like Lord Shiva, we were all born with a third eye. We use it spontaneously when we stand up selflessly and justly for the greater good. We are, after all, manifestations of the Creator, who created us in his own image, and like a benevolent father, allowed us to choose our own orbits.

The conundrums of birth, rebirth, life and death hound us perpetually. If we listened closely to the whispers of the universe, we may find the answers we seek. They often lie in the confines of our selves. Our teachers hover on the indiscernible fringes of our surroundings, but we are disinclined students.

The spirits try to guide us through their deeds or misdeeds, through sheer terror or subtle signs, through nightmare or dream. At the end of it all, we emerge stronger, wiser and transformed. It is imperative to uncover that elusive third eye to be able to see the potential for infinite learning outside our perceived limitations.

Consider the similarities in the paranormal encounters of people across the world. The translucent forms of spirits, the unyielding pressure on the chest when being preyed on, the white light of near death phenomena, the biting cold, the effect of a ghostly presence on electrical equipment, the slight yet perceptible change in a fresh corpse at the stage when the soul leaves the body. This cannot be a worldwide conspiracy theory or an uncontrolled epidemic accosting the imaginations of divergent human beings.

We have not seen God, yet we believe in him with unquestioning devotion. Why then do we scoff at the possibility of ghosts, instead of believing in the possibility of their existence at the very least? Why does blind faith desert us when faced with the idea of a spirit avatar?

This book is a journey into the unknown. It is an exploration of the transcendental bond, beyond that of mere blood, that ties family together. It is a mark of respect for dimensions that are outside our limited perception. It is the revelation that the living and the unliving may not reside in the same world but that they suffer the same vulnerabilities and sense of isolation. In spirits lies a wealth of spirituality.

This book had to be written.

It has to be shared.

It has to be believed.

It is where the spirits have led me – to you, to myself, to these chronicles.

Their stories and ours are one.

The message is clear.

The dead teach us to live.

Legacy

The kings of fright,
Will they surface at night?
Continuing their saga of fear,
Are those their spirits we hear?
Their movies will live on,
Even after the brothers have gone.
The masters of terror,
Was it destiny or error?

Acknowledgements

A book never belongs to one person alone. From the writer's mind to the reader's hands, many sleepless nights are spent in a creative collaboration. It is imperative to acknowledge the forces that assisted in giving birth to this labour of love.

My publishers and the team at HarperCollins India for believing in me. My amazing editor, Bushra Ahmed, for sharing my vision and making it a reality. My impeccable copyeditor, Ateendriya Gupta, for her invaluable input. And lastly, my dynamic literary agent, Anuj Bahri of Red Ink Literary Agency, for helping me reach for the stars and Sharvani Pandit for her considerable guidance

Then there are those who have helped me stay sane during the insane process of writing:

My sister, Jaya Thawani Jain, who has never given up on us or on her parental duties. My best friend who is family, Priya Sharma, for always being there. My friend, Satyarth Nayak, for his advice whenever needed. The walking encyclopedia of Ramsay horror, Dhruv Somani, for access to photographs, posters and information. And my wonderful in-laws, Poonam (Mummy), Mala, Pooja, Vijay, Millie, Ricky, Dipika and their families, for the constant encouragement.

Then there are the stalwarts of Bollywood that have helped so willingly without expectation: Dr Jayantilal Gada of PEN India Ltd and Mr Gordhan Tanwani of Baba Arts Ltd.

And above all, The Almighty, for bringing me this far.

Om Namah Shivay.
Jai Mata Di.

About the Author

Alisha Kirpalani is based in Mumbai, India. She is the daughter of Asha née Maya Ramsay and the granddaughter of F.U. Ramsay. From a young age Kirpalani knew of her family's history with the supernatural, and with this book she decided to document their memories and tales. She has previously authored two books; this is her first foray into non-fiction.